John Arthur Fraser

A Modern Ananias

A Comedy in Three Acts

John Arthur Fraser

A Modern Ananias
A Comedy in Three Acts

ISBN/EAN: 9783337054953

Printed in Europe, USA, Canada, Australia, Japan

Cover: Foto ©Andreas Hilbeck / pixelio.de

More available books at **www.hansebooks.com**

AUTHOR'S EDITION.

A MODERN ANANIAS

A COMEDY IN THREE ACTS,

BY

J. A. FRASER, Jr.,

Author of A Noble Outcast—Edelweiss—McGinty's Troubles—
Little Miss Mab—Esther's Guardeen—Inez—The Judge's
Wife—'Twixt Love and Money—The Merry Cob-
bler—Drafted—On Secret Service—
A Delicate Question—Etc.

CHICAGO:
THE DRAMATIC PUBLISHING COMPANY.

Cast of Characters.

Lysander Lyon, M. D. —With a vivid imagination.
Col. Lyon —With a forgiving disposition. Lysander's uncle.
Derby Dashwood -With a Piccadilly accent; Lysander's class-mate.
Francisco With an elastic conscience; Lysander's valet.
Baby—With the soubriquet of "Little Tootsywootsy"; Lysander's step-daughter.
Nellie Goldengate —With a fickle fancy; the Colonel's ward.
Prudence Mayflower - With New England notions; Nellie's friend.
Kittie—With so much a month and board; Baby's maid.

SCENE: - *Newport at the present time.*

ACT. I.   AFTERNOON **Lysander** *lies.*
ACT. II.   EVENING OF THE SAME DAY—*He continues to lie.*
ACT. III.   THE NEXT DAY --*The consequences.*

Reward.

I hereby offer a reward of $25.00 for the conviction of any actor pirating this piece and of $50.00 for the conviction of any manager permitting such piracy upon his stage.

J. A. FRASER, JR.,
DRAMATIC PUBLISHING CO.,
CHICAGO.

Author's Edition—Notice.

A MODERN ANANIAS.

Author's Notes.

To Amateurs in search of a comedy which is absolutely certain to provoke roars of laughter from beginning to end, *A Modern Ananias* is recommended with the utmost confidence. The situations into which the various characters are dragged through the mendacity of the hero are so intensely absurd in themselves and Lysander shows such wit and ingenuity in extricating himself and them until he is finally involved in a hopeless mass of tergiversation, that the piece positively plays itself. The only things absolutely essential are that the lines be carefully memorized, the stage directions minutely followed and that each actor play his or her part with full sincerity. To the audience, all the characters--no matter how funny the things they are doing or the lines they are speaking, must be in serious earnest with each other. The moment any consciousness of the ridiculous is shown, that moment the fun is lost. The personality of the actor must never overpower the personation of the character. This is the whole secret of successful farce playing.

It is rarely the case, even in farcical comedy, that so many distinctly drawn "fat" comedy parts are to be found. Lysander is the hero, it is true, but he has no advantage over the uncle, so far as part is concerned. Derby Dashwood comes in a hot second and as for Francisco, a clever player can get a laugh on every line he speaks. Baby, who may be with advantage played by a man, owing to the short-sighted objection of most young actresses to sacrificing personal charms to artistic success, is intensely funny. Nellie is a charming ingenue lead who gains the entire sympathy of the audience while Prudence and Kitty both show to good advantage the personal beauty and talent of the actresses who essay them: but Baby is the great part—almost the star.

The story is briefly this: Lysander Lyon was in his infancy deserted by his mother and taken care of by a bachelor uncle who grew immensely rich in California. Lysander is made his uncle's heir and goes to Europe to study. To inculcate economical habits he is restricted to a small allowance and meeting a rich widow, whose hold on life is slender, he marries her unknown to his uncle. After his marriage he finds himself step-father to a fleshy old maid to whom, on her mother's death, the expected fortune reverts. Meantime, the uncle has become guardian of Nellie Goldengate and decides that his two wards should marry. Unknown to Lysander he crosses the continent at a time when that young gentleman is paying a surreptitious visit to America. Lysander meets Nellie and scrapes acquaintance with her but, owing to Francisco's blunder, thinks her name is Prudence—the name of her friend. In order to avoid a marriage with Nellie, whom he thinks he has never seen, he invents a story to the effect that he is already married and then the complications ensue. Finally he is forced to confess all his deceptions except one—the truth about Baby. Nellie forgives him and so does the uncle for his fibs and also his first marriage but both imagine Baby to be a little child. Then the truth comes to the surface, when, by an almost superhuman effort of nerve, he marries his step-daughter to his uncle and himself weds Nellie.

While the main plot of *A Modern Ananias* is original with me, for many incidents I freely acknowledge my indebtedness—going back to the earliest record we have—to Lope de Vega. His comedy, "The Mistaken Beauty", (1661), was translated and adapted for the French stage by Corneille about thirty years later; turned into English from both sources by Dick Steele, 1703, adapted and modernized by Samuel Foote, 1762; and, more than a century later, again somewhat rewritten by Charles Mathews. A comedy that has been constantly on the stage for nearly 250 years must have strong elements of popularity; and readapted as whatever I have used of it is in *A Modern Ananias,* with the confessed weakness of the old comedy—lack of plot and complications, remedied, I modestly hope that my effort to render this fine old piece valuable to the present generation will not be without its reward. It is an interesting fact that Foote's adaptation of the comedy was running on the Covent Garden stage, London, during both our wars with England—1776, 1812. Interwoven with this piece is another, a farce by Charles Mathews, in which Edwin Booth appeared with great success in 1857. It is a curious fact that during his tour of America, Mr. Mathews played these two pieces for an evening's bill, and yet, apparently, never saw how each could be blended with the other. The plot of the story, as I tell it, is wholly original with me, as is most of the dialogue, while most of the old situations have been given a new lease of life by holding them up to the mirror of to-day.

Costumes.

Lysander. - First act, outing costume in the extreme of fashion. He should be made up dark and look about 24 years old. Second costume, full evening dress. Third act, cutaway black coat and vest, light pants, patent leather shoes. He is a dandy all through and must be played in sober earnest. **Col. Lyon,** is a big, red faced old man of sixty in exuberent health. White wig and side whiskers, grey suit and plug hat in first act; full evening dress in second act: Prince Albert and light pants, black silk hat and patent leather shoes in last act. **Derby Dashwood,** little curly-headed blonde with very dainty outing suit in first act; evening dress in second act and very dude tweed suit and straw hat in last act. **Francisco,** acts one and two, dark tweed suit, stiff felt hat; act three, livery. He must be made up very swarthy with coal black curly wig and coal black mustache. **Baby,** must look forty years old, be padded to look like 200 pounds and be gaudily dressed in styles suitable for a school-girl; ankle length skirts. Act one; burlesqued outing dress; act two, house dress with hair hanging down her back; act three the same. **Nellie** and **Prudence,** in act one, pretty outing dresses in the height of fashion. **Nellie** should be blonde and **Prudence** brunette. Act two, evening dress. For disguise **Nellie** should wear hat, thick veil and long, dark cape or mantle. Act three, summer morning dress, straw hats for both. **Kitty,** plain black dress, white apron, bonne's Normandy cap, white collar and cuffs.

Property Plot.

Act 1. Garden bench—eyeglass, newspaper and letter in envelope for Derby—address book and pencil for Lysander—letter in envelope for Francisco—Eyeglasses for Baby.

Act II. Large three-leaf screen—easel with picture—small fancy stand—carpet—fancy table with telegraph blanks and pen,ink and paper on it—sofa—four fancy chairs—Pack of cards—cribbage board—spectacles for Col. Lyon—thirteen cigars butts wrapped in paper for Baby.

Act III. Table with newspaper on it—five chairs—sofa—carpet—sideboard with decanter containing cold tea, glasses and pitcher of water on it—revolver—broom, dustpan, fourteen cigar butts for Kitty—cigars for Derby and Col. Lyon—three flowers in pots for Francisco—Artificial cut flowers for Baby—child's lace hood for Nellie—jumping jack for Col Lyon.

A MODERN ANANIAS.
SCENE PLOTS.

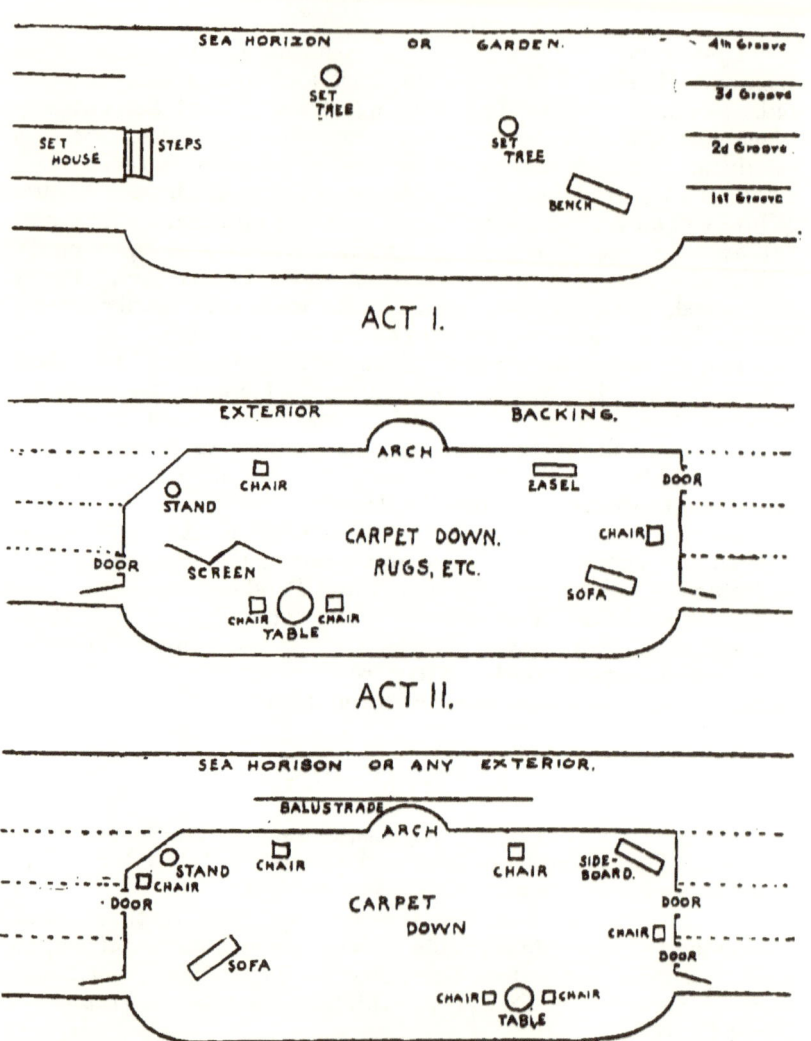

ACT I.

ACT II.

ACT III.

A MODERN ANANIAS.

ACT I.

[SCENE: *Newport. Sea horizon or garden drop at fourth grooves. Set tree C. at back. Set tree L. C. at second grooves. Garden bench down L. Set house with steps* R. 2 E. *Wood wings and foliage borders. Set house represents a hotel. At rise of curtain* **Derby** *enters* R. U. E. *with* **Nellie** *on his* R. *arm and* **Prudence** *on his* L. *They speak as they enter and come down to bench* L.]

Nell.   How dreadfully slow it is at Newport this summer.

Derb.   Yes, awfully! On account of the hard times, don't you know.   Oh, I say—some new people have moved into the lower flat of our villa.

Prud.   I do hope there are men among them and dancing men at that.

Derb.   Oh, yes—two men—quite knowable looking fellows, they tell me.

Nell.   Thank heaven for small mercies!   We girls are prepared to tolerate almost anything that wears   [*Sitting on bench.*]

Prud.   [L. C.] Ahem!   Nellie!

Nell.   Bifurcated garments.   But who and what are they?

Derb.   Don't know, really.   [L. C.]

Nell.   Ascertain their names, position, and the state of their bank accounts within fifteen minutes or prepare to suffer—Eh, Prudie?

Prud.   I should say so—and particularly whether they are married or single.   We'll wait for you here.   [*Sits on bench* L.]

Derb.   But by Jove! you know a fellow can't find out all that in fifteen minutes.

Nell.   No excuses—if you're not back in a quarter of an hour—
[*Gallops off* L. I. E.]

Derb.   The flag has dropped.   They're off, with Dashwood in the lead.   [*Galloping off* L. I. E.]

Nell.   He's a good little soul, but quite impossible.   [*Laughing.*]

Prud.   Why, I was prepared to see you

Nell. Marry him? Ha, ha, ha! [*Rises and goes* c.] A two thousand dollar ninth assistant something or other at Washington?

Prud. How can you trifle so with a man's affections, Nellie? I'd feel positively guilty.

Nell. You're altogether too innocent for this wicked world, my dear. Besides he's used to it. [*Looks off* R. I. E.] Oh—what a handsome fellow!.

Prud. [*Rises and goes* c. *looking off*.] Two of them—what a shame we don't know them!

Nell. [R. C.] Give them a chance and they'll introduce themselves. [*Flutters handkerchief*.]

Prud. For heaven's sake Nellie! what will they *think* of us?

Nell. What will *we* think of them?—that's the point. I'll spread a net. [*Drops handkerchief. Goes* L. *and sits on bench*.]

Prud. Then you'll have to excuse *me*. [*Retiring up behind tree* L.]

[*Enter* **Lysander** *and* **Francisco** R. I. E.]

Lys. [*Crossing* L.] Pardon me Miss—Permit me to restore your handkerchief.

Nell. Oh, thank you so much! How stupid of me to have dropped it.

Lys. [L. C. **Frans.** R. C.] A most happy accident for me. Chance has given me an honor in one lucky minute that my utmost diligence has been unable to procure in the whole round of a revolving year.

Nell. You must be mistaken, sir.

Lys. Ah, if I only were! Surely you must have remarked my respectful assiduity—every play, opera, ball or banquet where I thought there was the slightest chance of seeing you I have haunted like your own shadow. I have even loitered about your door and followed you to Newport in despair. [*Sits beside her* **Prud.** *peeps from behind tree*.]

Fran. [*Aside*.] Heavens what gall.

Lys. Ever since my return from South America I have daily risked arrest by following you with my mute but respectful homage.

Fran. [*Aside*.] Oh, what a liar!

Nell. [*Aside*.] Strange that I never noticed him. He really is a most fascinating man. [*Aloud*.] Then you have visited South America?

Lys. I know every foot of it. During the late attempt to restore monarchical rule in Brazil I shed my blood in defense of the sister Republic.

Nell. You were wounded?

Lys. Shot all to pieces [*Rises.*] There wasn't a battle of any consequence but I had an opportunity to distinguish myself. The final rout of the insurgents and the seizure of their vessels was considered a master-stroke of genius. The President wrote me a personal letter of thanks.

Nell. I have heard the honor of that undertaking ascribed to some native general.

Lys. Doubtless, but you can't believe the newspapers. History, if a Portugese can write *history* as distinguished from *romance*, will do me justice. But I don't expect it. No Portugese can tell the truth.

Fran. [*Aside.*] What an excellent Portugese he'd make!

Lys. But pardon me allow me to present my friend, Don Francisco Martinez, a Brazilian by birth, an insurgent by profession and an American citizen by naturalization. [**Nell.** *rises* **Fran.** *crosses* L. *and they both bow deeply. She makes room on the bench and* **Fran.** *sits beside her.*]

Nell. [*Aside.*] Don Francisco! He must be noble. How lovely!

Lys. [c.] The Don and I have been sworn friends since I had the honor of saving his precious life. He was among the prisoners taken by our army after I had fustrated an attempt of the enemy to enter Rio. He was tried by court martial and speedily sentenced to be shot at noon. Too proud of the blood of his noble race to sue for mercy he stood there calmly, folded his arms and said, "Bring forth your gattling guns, order up your artillery I will show you how an American citizen can die." On hearing these noble words I mounted my horse and galloped madly to our minister's official residence- --

Nell. [*Rises excitedly*, L. c.] And saved him? How thrilling!

Lys. [c.] Alas! Our minister had gone a-fishing. The case was desperate. In five minutes the sun-parched soil of Brazil would be greedily drinking up the life-blood of a fearless and patriotic American citizen--by naturalization. Snatching the glorious emblem of our nation from where it proudly floated above the door, I remounted my horse, dashed wildly to the plaza where the firing party stood drawn up and poor Don Francisco was gazing with a sickly palor upon his face into the deadly muzzles of thirteen repeating rifles. Spurring my horse I broke a passage through a troop of cavalry and forced a battalion of infantry aside. Riding like a lunatic between the firing party and their devoted victim, I flung the Star Spangled Banner to the breeze and enveloped him in its folds. "Fire on that flag if you dare!" I shouted, "If you do you fire on seventy millions of people who will swarm down here within twenty-four hours and whip you out of your boots."

Nell. How noble! How daring! [*Goes c. to him.*]

Lys. Wasn't it? Recoginizing that I had cleverly avoided war with the United States by my prompt action, the President was lavish in his praise and made me a general.

Nell. A general! [*Gives her hand. He conducts her across* R.]

Lys. [*Crossing.*] But ah, Miss—the battle scarred warrior is vanquished at last and happier in his defeat than in triumphing over a battlefield red with carnage. If you but smile upon me—-

Nell. [R. C.] Why—General- —

Lys. Now don't spring that old gag—"This is so sudden" they all say that—

Nell. But, General-

Lys. At least indulge me with your address, both here and at home. [*Takes out book.*]

Nell. What give my address to a gentleman who for a whole year has stood sentinel at my doorstep? Ha, ha, ha! [**Prnd.** *crosses* R. *to steps.*]

Lys. My dear young lady—you misunderstand—let me explain——

Nell. Ha, ha, ha! Not another word. Your nerve is exquisite Good morning, general—general disaster, ha, ha, ha! [*Ex. into hotel with* **Prud.**]

Lys. General disaster? The deuce! I should say it was. [*Goes c.*]

Fran. [*Joining him c.*] That was a bad break, sir.

Lys. I'll mend it. She's a stunner and I've mashed her.

Fran. I wish you had mashed the other one for me! But see here, sir my conscience is elastic enough, heaven knows, yet that life saving yarn was almost *too* much. Why did you tell it?

Lys. Because I've got to interest a rich woman. She looked rich and I interested her.

Fran. But your uncle has picked out a wife for you.

Lys. Nellie Goldengate—his ward and I've never seen her. [*Crosses* L. *and sits.*]

Fran. [L. C.] You're not taking any more chances than she is.

Lys. Besides, if he should find out about my little speculation of six months ago I'd be done for so far as he is concerned.

Fran. What did you invest in a mine?

Lys. No—a widow of sixty with one foot in the grave and two hundred and fifty thousand in the bank

Fran. What—feet?

Lys. No, dollars. After my marriage I found that I also had a step-daughter.

Fran. And such a step-daughter!

Lys. After two short months of wedded bliss, which seemed like twenty years, she got the other foot into the grave. But the season of my joy—I mean my grief, was short. My step-daughter inherited the $250,000. It was a cruel, cruel blow. I've had to put up with my dear child's whims from that day to this—or go round without enough money to buy cigars.

Fran. But to return to my conscience, sir; I've noticed that you are rather given to stretching things.

Lys. You insinuate that I'm a liar.

Fran. Well, you do embellish, a bit. Now, for instance—I never was in Brazil in all my life.

Lys. No more was I.

Fran. But this lady will give it out that you are a general in the Brazilian army.

Lys. And make me so much the more interesting to every heiress in Newport.

Fran. But you may be found out.

Lys. Brazil is a long way off. Who is there to contradict me?

Fran. Your step-daughter.

Lys. Oh, darn my step-daughter! [*Rises and goes c.*] I'll manage *her.* You go and find out that young lady's name and all about her.

Fran. I won't be a minute, sir. [*Ex. into hotel R. 2 E.*]

[*Enter* **Kitty** L. 1. E.]

Lys. Ah, Kitty—where is my little girl?

Kitty. [L.] She isn't up yet.

Lys. [c.] Is she asleep?

Kitty. I don't think she ever sleeps. This morning she's in one of her tempers, calling me everything she can lay her tongue to.

Lys. Oh, you mustn't mind her.

Kitty. [*Going c. to him.*] But I *do* mind her and I've come to give in my notice. I can't stand her any longer. She's old enough to know better, so she is. [*Indignantly goes a little L.*]

Lys. She *is* old enough, but remember her temper is considered in your wages.

Kitty. [*Turning confidentially L. c.*] I leave it to you, sir. Is it my fault that she can't make her corset meet? Does that give her any call to fire the soap dish at my head and fetch me a soaker with a wet sponge?

Lys. Baby *is* growing a trifle stout, but you agreed to put up with that for so much a month and your board.

Kitty. Oh, Lord, sir! Here she comes. [*Starts to run* R. U. E.]

Lys. [*Detains her.*] Don't run away—stand your ground. [*Looks off* L. I. E.] Sweet little thing. [*Retires up behind tree* C.]

[*Enter Baby* L. I. E.]

Baby. [*Down* L.] Oh you stupid, clumsy, ignorant thing! I've been searching everywhere for you. Who was that man? You scandalous huzzy! Oh, how I hate you! [*Stamps angrily.*]

Lys. Baby, I'm ashamed of you. [*Reappearing.*]

Baby. [*Putting on eyeglasses.*] Oh, papa! Is it really you? Good morning, dear papa. [*Hippity-hops up to him.*]

Lys. [*Aside.*] Papa—papa. Nice isn't it? But I've got to stand it!

Baby. Kiss your baby good morning, papa. What are you angry with poor little me? Have I been naughty? [*Drawing him down* C.]

Lys. Naughty? Oh no darling no pet. Come and kiss its daddy. [*Kiss. Aside.*] How absurd!

Baby. [R. C. *down stage.*] I was so afraid I was in disgrace, papa—and I was going—I was going to ask a favor.

Lys. [C.] What favor, dear? [**Kitty** *drops down* L.]

Baby. [*Timidly.*] If—if I may go out.

Lys. Of course you may, my child. Go out as much as you like. [*Aside.*] Go out and get lost in the crowd.

Baby. But I'm so afraid of the *mashers*, papa. [*Clinging to him timidly.*]

Lys. They'd never think of molesting my little Tootsywootsy. [*Goes a little* L.]

Baby. [C.] But don't you want to know where I am going, papa?

Lys. Oh, go to the——[*She starts away* R.] Hold on I've changed my mind. I won't have you gadding about, Miss. [*Aside.*] What nonsense! A woman of her age playing the child. That's one of her whims!

Baby. Oh papa! I only want to go to the florist's to buy some fresh roses for my vases.

Lys. [L. C. *Aside.*] Fresh roses for her *vaw-ses*! [*Aloud.*] Well, that's different. [*Looks at watch.*] Let me see—you may be gone just five hours. But don't stop a single minute over your time or papa will be very angry.

Baby. Won't you go with me, papa?

Lys. Impossible, pet. I have business of the utmost importance.

Baby. What business. papa?

Lys. [*Pause.*] I've got to get shaved.

Baby. [*Goes* R. *Sobbing.*] Oh—I see—that's only an excuse. I'm a drag on you—a tie—a burden.

Lys. [*Following her.*] Now, now Tootsywootsy—I don't mean that.

Baby. [R.] Yes you do—you know you do. Well, there is one very simple way of getting rid of me.

Lys. [R.] There is? Spring it quick.

Baby. Marry me off.

Lys. Yes—yes love. Oh, that's dead easy. There's plenty of time—I'll see about it. [*Returning* C.]

Baby. Selfish, selfish papa! You want to keep your little girl all to yourself.

Lys. [*Aside.*[Oh, I do—I do—not. [*Aloud.*] Go dear—Kitty will take care of you—there's no danger. [*Kitty crosses up* R.]

Baby. No danger in Newport? Then what did I come here for? No danger! [*Goes up a little.*]

Lys. [C.] Not in broad daylight, my precious. Now at night, if the electric lights went out, perhaps—

Baby. But the rude men positively stare a girl out of countenance——

Lys. [*Aside.*] I'd pay a bonus if they would only stare her out of *her* countenance. [*Aloud.*] Now run along, your Kittywitty is waiting for you, pet.

Baby. I always do as you tell me, don't I papa?

Lys. You do. [*Aside.*] When you feel like it.

Baby. [*To* Kitty.] Now then, you lazy thing—I wish I had my carriage here, papa.

Kitty. [*Aside going.*] Pretty dear! They ought to buy her a bicycle. [*Ex.* R. 3 E.]

Baby. Well, good-by, papa dear, and thank you. [*Coming down to him.*]

Lys. [*Impatiently.*] Oh—good-by——

Baby. [R. C.] Don't you want to kiss your Baby? That check you asked for——[*Shows a check.*]

Lys. [C.] My child! [*Kisses her.*] Child indeed!

Baby. [*Gives check.*] Ta, ta, papa dear. [*Goes* R. 3 E.]

Lys. [*Disgusted.*] Oh tata, tata. [*Ex.* Baby R. 3 E.] Go to the devil!

[*Enter* Derby L. 1. E.. *tears newspaper angrily.*]

Lys. Hello! what the deuce is up with this fellow? Why, it's Dashwood, my old class-mate at Yale. [*Crosses* L. *slaps* Derby *on* *shoulder.* **Fran.** *enters from hotel.*]

Derb. *Don't* do that! [*Puts up eyeglass.*]   What the devil do you mean by it?

Lys. Why Derby, old boy, don't you remember me? Lysander Lyon.

Derb. Oh, to be sure, dear fellow. How de do. [*Shake hands high up in the air.*]

Lys. What has ruffled you?

Derb. A report in this confounded paper about some mysterious stranger with a weakness for a certain young lady, don't you know. [*Sits L.*]

Lys. [L. C.] Who is the lady?

Derb. They've reversed her initials to G. N. from N. G., but I recognize her.

Lys. Oh—she's N. G. [*Winks at audience.*]

Derb. Last night, don't you know, he gave a water party.

Lys. Swell party?

Derb. Awfully select, really. The young lady and a friend and himself and a friend.

Lys. Good time?

Derb. Steam yacht decorated with flowers, string band, high priced quartet and supper at $100 a plate—Oh awfully—cost him a small fortune!

Lys. And you don't know who the man is?

Derb. Can't even guess. That's what makes me feel so devilish.

Lys. Ha, ha, ha! Well—I might as well plead guilty.

Derb. What, *you?* [*Rising incredulously.*]

Lys. Yes—I. Why not?

Fran. [R. *Aside.*] He's at it again

Derb. Then you're the new man at Arlington villa!

Lys. Exactly. But don't breathe a word about my identity. I like mystery.

Derb. I can keep a secret. [*Aside.*] My rival, by Jove! He doesn't suspect that I'm his upstairs. I'll watch him.. [*Crossing to R. C.*]

Lys. [*Reading paper.*] Ha, ha! How the deuce do these newspaper fellows manage to get hold of things?

Derb. The fellows who do them usually write out a full account and send it to the editor by special messenger. But you're a lucky fellow—only a few days back from dear old England and favored by the biggest heiress of the season, by Jove!

Lys. Why, man, I've been back six weeks but my presence is a secret. Uncle Dick would be furious if he found it out. You know him?

Derb. Oh, yes—I've met the Colonel. He told me something of your queer history, don't you know.

Lys. Odd, isn't it? You see, he was already in California when my father married and was subsequently divorced on perjured testimony. Then my mother married before her decree got cold. In a fit of depression my father blew his brains out and Uncle Dick adopted me on the condition that I should never recognize my mother. He hates her although he never saw her.

Derb. Quite a romance, by Jove!

Lys. As for the old gentleman, he's safe in Frisco and fondly imagines that I'm at Guy's Hospital, London. [*Sits* L.]

Derb. [c. *Aside.*] He doesn't know the old boy is here! I won't do a *thing to him*—oh no! By Jove! [*Aloud.*] Well, old fellow, I'll have to move along, don't you know.

Lys. What's your hurry?

Derb. I have an appointment, really. [*Going* R.]

Lys. Don't tear yourself away—sit down and let me tell you about my trip abroad.

Derb. Another time, old man—I really must go—ta, ta—jolly girl, N. G., lucky fellow—bye, bye. [*Ex. into hotel.*]

Fran. May I ask a question, sir? [*Crossing* L.]

Lys. Sure thing.

Fran. [L. c.] Where do you smoke?

Lys. Smoke? Any place, if there are no ladies present.

Fran. But I mean where do you go to hit the pipe?

Lys. Oh, go to the devil. [*Rises and takes* c.]

Fran. I didn't think you were so stuck on it as that; but you do have the gaudiest lot of pipe dreams I ever heard of.

Lys. [*Turning angrily.*] You quit my service to-night.

Fran. [L. c. *coolly.*] Not on your life. I like the place.

Lys. I've a good mind to knock you down.

Fran. I can do my own knocking down. I was once a bartender. See here, sir, if you don't lie yourself into some infernal scrape I'll be content to be hanged.

Lys. If I do and don't lie myself out again I'll be content to be shot. You mind your own business. Did you find out about that charming girl?

Fran. I did. She is Prudence Mayflower of Boston and her father has made a million in chewing gum.

Lys. [c.] What a lot of gum he must have chewed. Is she single?

Fran. Engaged.

Lys. Then I'll marry her.

Fran. If she's engaged?

Lys. Sure thing. I make it a practice never to marry a girl who *isn't* engaged. [*Voices heard in hotel.*] Hark! I know that voice. By all that's unlucky it's Uncle Dick. [*Looking in door. Crosses* L.]

Fran. Duck, sir, duck—behind the trees, quick!

Lys. Too late—he sees me. I was a fool not to vanish the moment I heard him. [*Col. and Derby appear at door.*]

Fran. Your friend is with him. What are you going to do?

Lys. Stand my ground and lie out of it. If you know when you're well off you'll back up every thing I say. [*Sits* L.]

Fran. [L. C.] You tell the lies. I'll swear to them.

Lys. Not a word about my marriage or step-daughter.

Fran. Mum's the word.

Lys. If I pull through I'll set up a case.

Fran. A case, sir? Give me a tip.

Lys. Sure. If you're quiet, a case of Mumm. Here he comes. [*Fran. retires up.*]

Col. [*Enters* R. 2 E. *and comes down steps.*] Well, sir, what the thunder are you doing *here.* [*Crossing* L.]

Lys. [*Rising.*] Returning the compliment, Uncle, what the thunder are *you* doing here?

Col. I thought you were in England. [*Angrily.*]

Lys. I thought you were in California. [*Quietly.*]

Col. You're an ungrateful, undutiful scamp.

Lys. Not I, sir. I came here to see you. [*Crossing* C.]

Col. Why aren't you dosing and carving people at Guy's Hospital?

Lys. I couldn't stand the climate—contracted chronic bronchitis complicated with regurgitation of the liver. I thought I was going to croke and my doctors ordered a sea voyage and change of air.

Col. Hum! That's why you've been home six weeks without letting me know it. [*Sits* L. *on bench.*]

Lys. I only arrived in New York yesterday and came straight to Newport to pay my respects.

Col. Too thin, sir. I am better informed—you have been in America six weeks and I know it.

Lys. You have been grossly deceived, sir. [*Beckons to* **Fran.** *who comes down.*] Let me present you to Don Francisco Martinez—a Brazilian nobleman.

Col. Proud to meet you, Don. [*Rising and bowing.*]

Fran. [L. C.] I have much pleasure. [*Bowing profoundly, raising hat with a flourish.*]

Lys. [C.] Don Francisco will tell you that we were fellow passengers on the Britannic and arrived in New York yesterday.

Fran. Oh, that is certain!

Col. [*Perplexed.*] Well—I'm dashed! From the same source I hear that you are wildly infatuated with some woman. [*Crosses to Lys.* c.]

Lys. Sir!

Col. And that last night you gave her certain recklessly extravagant proofs that you are a fool, sir.

Lys. *I* did, Uncle? How?

Col. Steam yachts, string bands, bushels of flowers, opera singers and the Lord knows what all!

Lys. [R. c.] What an absurd lie! You know the state of my finances too well to believe a word of it. Who told you?

Col. A friend of yours. He knows it all.

Lys. Dashwood! He always knows it all. Moreover he is here and is likewise the most notorious liar of my acquaintance.

Col. I am astounded—what, Dashwood a liar?

Lys. Joe Mulhatton's only living rival. I had to cut his acquaintance because I innocently repeated a few common-place things he told me. People actually began to accuse *me* of untruthfulness.

Fran. [L.] [*Aside.*] How cruel.

Col. I never heard this of him before.

Lys. Do you want any stronger proof than this silly lie? What's more, I'll bet his description was as detailed as it was vivid.

Col. It was; extremely so.

Lys. [R. c.] That's his system. He'd deceive the very elect. Why, there isn't a scintilla of truth in the whole story. Is there Don?

Fran. [L. c.] All absolute fiction, upon my honor. I'll swear to that.

Col. I've been imposed upon. Yet I can't help pitying the fellow—he's very agreeable company. [*Crossing* L.]

Lys. Liars usually *are* entertaining.

Col. [L.] That's a fact. And when they once contract the habit they can't reform. It becomes constitutional.

Lys. Dashwood's case to a dot. [*Crossing* L.]

Fran. [*Aside.*] I'll swear it's his! [*Crossing* R.]

Col. Well, sir, I'm glad you have been able to explain this thing. Now I must be off to find my doctor.

Lys. You're not ill, I hope?

Col. I'm a very sick man. Came all the way from California to consult Dr. Soakem, the eminent specialist.

Lys. [L. c.] Why, what's the matter?

Col. [L.] I don't know. I wish I did. Dr. Briggs doesn't know either and I'm afraid I'm in a very bad way. Just imagine —whenever I eat—I may even say sometimes when I don't eat, I have such a feeling of fullness all down here and all through here —

Lys. How many meals do you eat a day?

Col. Very seldom more than three.

Lys. You're in a very critical condition. As a medical man I tell you that.

Col. This is what I feared. I have sent for my attorney who will be here to-morrow to make my will. Meantime I want to introduce you to a girl.

Lys. [*Aside.*] That awful girl from California!

Col. Where can I meet you in an hour?

Lys. Anywhere you please, sir.

Col. Then right here.

Lys. Very well, sir. In an hour.

Col. Don Francisco, I bid you good day, sir. If there is anything I can do for you I shall be most happy, sir.

Fran. [R. c.] I thank you with all my heart.

[*Ex. Col. L. 2 E.*]

Lys. [*Shaking hands with Fran.*] You get the champagne, I've squared myself and knocked Dashwood's eye out all at one stroke. Derby's a knocker but I carry a nice long-handled hammer myself. [*Goes up a little c.*]

Fran. You'll have an awful time reconciling those stories some day.

Lys. [*Up c.*] Not if I quit now. Of course if I keep up this clip in the course of time my reputation for veracity may actually be questioned and I couldn't stand that. I have told my last fib. From this moment I'm a reformed man! Dull, prosaic truth is my long suit and my rampant imagination is curbed with an intellectual bit and bridle! [*This brings him R. c. up.*]

Fran. [R.] Noble resolution.

Lys. Now for that lovely girl. I must write her a letter and lay my heart at her feet.

Fran. You're not losing any time.

Lys. Strike while the iron's hot, Francisco. Never let a woman forget you, even for a minute. Let's see—what the deuce is her name? Tutti Frutti.

Fran. Well, hardly!

Lys. I know it has something to do with chewing gum.

Fran. Her father made his million in gum.

Lys. Sure—and that accounts for the way he stuck to his money. But her name?

Fran. Prudence Mayflower.

Lys. That's it. Lovely name. Prudence Mayflower! Puts you in mind of the Pilgrim fathers, Plymouth Rock, Back Bay, Bunker Hill and all that sort of thing. Well, I'll write her a letter without a single lie in it.

Fran. That's right, sir. Tell the truth -for a change.

Lys. It would be ungenerous to deceive a lady, particularly one whose papa has waggled a million dollars out of people's jaws by the chewing gum route. Come, I want you to carry my letter. [*Ex. L. U. E.*]

Fran. I'd like to read that romance when its written. *Ex. L. U. E.*]

Enter **Nell.** *and* **Prud.** *from hotel. They speak as they cross* L.

Prud. Are you really smitten with that adventurer, dear?

Nell. Adventurer he may be; but he is a very charming fellow.

Prud. Beware how you throw away yourself and your fortune on a man you know nothing about except from his own account.

Nell. I'd sooner throw myself away than be thrown by my guardian into the arms of his precious nephew. Ugh! I hate doctors! [*Sits and does fancy work.*]

Prud. Then poor Derby Dashwood's nose is out of joint.

Nell. Not necessarily.

Prud. What are your intentions?

Nell. I haven't any. Perhaps, if I don't like this stranger better, I may marry Derby yet. I may even marry Dr. Lyon, but I'd hate to do it.

Prud. I'm afraid you're a very giddy girl, dear.

Nell. On the contrary—I'm strictly business. For instance, I have invested my money in a variety of stocks, bonds and other properties. If one investment goes up the flume, I still have the others to fall back on.

Prud. But what has that to do with matrimony? [*Sits further up stage on bench.*]

Nell. Oh, it's *distinctly* a matter o' money—now, you wouldn't have me more careful of my purse than of my person and for that reason I don't put all my matrimonial eggs into one basket, either.

Prud. Oh! I see, dear. You have invested your love in a variety of masculine securities.

Nell. Precisely. The visible supply of husbands consists of the stranger, Derby Dashwood and Dr. Lyon. I am prepared to hate that gentleman on sight but I had to invest in him too in order to corner the husband market.

Prud. [*Aside.*] Well, of all the conceit! [*Rising and going c.*]

[*Enter* **Col.** L. 2 E. *He goes c. to* **Prud.** *and then to* **Nell.**

Col. [*Kisses their hands.*] An old man's privilege my dears. I have news for you Nellie.

Nell. News for me?

Col. [*Going c. as* **Prud.** *crosses* L.] Yes. Lysander has returned hastily from Europe in consequence of a bad case of liver---I mean bronchitis. He is in Newport.

Nell. [*To Prud.*] The battle is on.

Col. Eh--what? My dear, as I've told you before, nothing would please me so much as your marriage to my nephew, but I'll never force your inclinations.

Nell. [*Aside.*] You bet you won't!

[**Fran.** *enters* L. U. E. *with note, cautiously crosses to hotel, exits, reappears and exits again* L. U. E.]

Col. Well, I really must be off to see that specialist--Dr. Soakem--a very clever man. Just imagine--whenever I eat, and indeed I may say---

Nell. Oh, we are familiar with the symptoms, Guardy--ha, ha, ha!

Col. So you are--I had forgotten. Don't forget, Miss Prudence, that you promised me a game of cribbage after dinner. Till then, au revoir.

Prud. I'll not forget--au revoir. [*Ex.* **Col.** L. U. E.] What a dear old man!

Nell. Indeed he is, but for all that I'm not going to marry Lysander. [*Enter* **Derb.** *from hotel*] Why, what's the matter with Derby?

Prud. He looks as if he had a pain.

Derb. [*Crossing* L.] A letter for you Miss Mayflower. I saw it in your box and thought you might like to have it at once, don't you know.

Prud. Thank you very much. Will you excuse me? [*Retires up and opens letter. Makes strenuous efforts to overhear the conversation.* **Nell.** *observes this.*]

Derb. [L. C.] I hope you feel no ill effects from last night's dissipation, Miss Goldengate.

Nell. Dissipation?

Derb. I was afraid you might have taken cold through staying so late on the water, don't you know.

Nell. What are you talking about?

Derb. Steam yacht, operatic concert, flowers, dancing don't you know, and supper at a hundred dollars a plate. Irresistible temptation to late hours, really

Nell. [*Aside.*] Poor little man. His brain is turned.

Derb. [*Aside.*] She winces. [*Aloud.*] I suppose you are charmed with Dr. Lyon. Such a jolly, dashing, altogether desirable fellow, to say nothing of his lavish hospitality, don't you know.

Nell. You really ought to carry an umbrella. The sun has such an awful effect on some people.

Derb. That doesn't answer my question about Lyon, don't you know.

Nell. I never give my opinion of a man I don't know—don't you know.

Derb. You don't know Lysander Lyon?

Nell. Never saw him in my life.

Derb. Really!

Nell. [*Rises. Very angry. Pauses a moment and then cuttingly.*] You insult me, Mr. Dashwood.

Derb. I beg pardon, really. [*Aside.*] Who would imagine that those lips could utter such diabolical crammers, by Jove! [*Aloud.*] Miss Goldengate, do you know that one of us is about to cut a very ridiculous figure?

Nell. Don't worry. I'm not going to cut you, Mr. Dashwood.,

Derb. Nobody ever doubted your wit, Miss Goldengate; but I repeat—one of us is about to look very foolish.

Nell. Nobody ever doubted your talent for excelling in that direction, Mr. Dashwood.

Derb. Thanks, awfully, but it doesn't chance to fall to my lot on this occasion, don't you know.

Nell. Oh—*I* am to play the fool! How amusing! Ha, ha, ha! But really, I am so dull that I can't make head or tail of this funny little spat.

Derb. [c. *very pompously.*] Allow me to inform you, then, that I am fully aware of last night's revels.

Nell. How dreadful! [*Mockingly.*]

Derb. From the moment you boarded the yacht until you landed at daybreak I know every detail.

Nell. You terrify me.

Derb. Yes—opera singers, musicians, cut flowers and Delmonico supper. I know it all.

Nell. You always *do* know it all. How did you find it out?

Derb. From the lips of the very idiot whose folly provided such a display of lavish extravagance.

Nell. His name. I demand it. [*With suppressed rage, stepping towards him*]

Derb. [*Retreating a little* R.] Lysander Lyon, M. D.

Nell. He told you all this himself? [*Still advancing. He retreats* R.]

Derb. He did.

Nell. You didn't fall asleep and dream it?

Derb. Most certainly not.

Nell. Then I don't know what Dr. Lyon was thinking of. [*Sweeps around and goes* L.]

Derb. [R.] Cornered at last, by Jove!

Nell. [*Turns suddenly.*] Not at all, sir. And as you can hardly expect me to be very much delighted with this visit you will excuse me wishing it as brief as possible. [*Sits* L.]

Derb. [*Crossing to* C.] I am not surprised that you feel embarrased, Miss Goldengate, and for the future I shall do myself the pleasure, don't you know, of sparing you the annoyance of my presence. Good afternoon.

Nell. Thanks, awfully. Good afternoon. [*Exit* Derb. L. U. E. Prud. *comes down!*] Well, did you ever hear the equal of that!

Prud. [C.] Of course I couldn't help hearing part of the conversation.

Nell. Of *course* you couldn't, dear. [*Somewhat sarcastically.*]

Prud. And you really never saw Dr. Lyon?

Nell. You know I didn't.

Prud. Then lose no time in making his acquaintance, dear. [*With malicious sweetness.*]

Nell. Why so, Prudie?

Prud. Don't call me Prudie, I hate it.

Nell. Dear Miss Mayflower—why should I lose no time in making Dr. Lyon's acquaintance?

Prud. Because he's your last chance.

Nell. Ha, ha, ha! Oh, I *guess* not! But what have you there?

Prud. A letter from the general whom we met this morning.

Nell. *We* met! That's *good!* What does he say? Oh, I beg your pardon, I didn't mean to ask.

Prud. I have no secrets from you, dear. [*Sits beside her.*] It's merely a formal declaration of love.

Nell. Why, you didn't even see him.

Prud. Oh, yes I did. What is more, he very evidently saw me. You may read it.

Nell. [*Glancing at letter.*] Carried by storm—artillery of your eyes—heart's undying devotion—forced to capitulate—fortress of your affections—hand and fortune at your feet. The stranger. Why, it's addressed to *you.*

Prud. Of *course* it is. [*Triumphantly.*]

Nell. But he signs no name.

Prud. There was no need. [*Rises.*] Our eyes met and we understood each other. [*Rapturously.*]

Nell. [*Ironically.*] Let me congratulate you, dear, on your conquest. [*Rises and kisses her. Aside.*] Hateful thing. She always was homely and conceited, but since she is growing old she is becoming a perfect fright.

Prud. [*Who has gone up c. Looking off* L. U. E.] Why, Nell, here come the general and his Brazilian friend with Col. Lyon.

Nell. You don't say. Let me have a peep. [*Going up. Looks off.*] They're coming here.

Prud. It won't do to meet him in your guardian's presence.

Nell. Hardly. It would involve some awkward explanation.

Prud. They come—we've no time to lose. [*Exit into hotel.*]

[*Enter* Col., Lys, *and* Fran, L. U. E.]

Col. [*As they come down.*] Ah, Don, you have been so entertaining that I forgot all about my specialist again. Oh, well, to-morrow will be time enough. I don't suppose I'm in any immediate danger. [Fran. *goes down* R.]

Lys. [R. C.] You'd better put yourself under my treatment, uncle.

Col. [C.] Not on purpose, my boy. No experiments for me. I want a man who knows his business.

Lys. Have your own way—it's your money to waste as you will.

Col. My boy, I'll put you onto something. The fellow who like Dr. Soakem won't even look at your tongue for less than a hundred dollars in advance gets a man's confidence, and confidence is everything. But what's the matter with you? There's something on your mind. [*Drawing him* L.]

Lys. Nothing, uncle, I assure you.

Col. Don't tell me. You don't seem a bit enthusiastic over marrying a lovely girl with money to burn and good, sound, common sense into the bargain.

Lys. There's plenty of time for marriage, sir. I don't want to settle down just yet.

Col. There isn't plenty of time, sir. Nell has a whole herd of lovers dangling about and the first thing you know one of them will snap her up. [*Sits.*]

Lys. [L. C.] [*Aside.*] I wish one of them would. He'd have *my* blessing.

Col. Haven't I always done what was best for you? Very well. I'm going to handle this matter on business principles. You shall commence courting her to-night or by jingo, yes—by the *living*

jingo I'll cut you off with a silver dollar to buy a rope to hang
yourself.

Lys.   But Miss Goldengate may object to being courted on business principles.

Col.   No she won't, sir. I've educated her up to it.

Lys.   Then I may not like her.

Col.   Don't you dare to come and tell *me* you don't like her or
you'll see trouble. I do everything on a system. This is Satur-
day. You begin courting her to-night. I'll help you.

Lys.   You're very kind.

Col.   To-morrow will be Sunday and you'll take a day off --to
court her. Again I'll help you. Monday night you'll propose to
her.

Lys.   Will you help me?

Col.   No sir. You'll have to go it alone. She's a sensible girl
and she'll accept. This day week you shall marry her.

Lys.   Will you help me.

Col.   [*Rises.*] Oh, don't be an ass! Now, remember these
are my wishes and I make my will to-morrow. [*Crossing to c.*]

Lys.   Then you are resolved?

Col.   Fixed.

Lys.   Positively?

Col.   Immovably.

Lys.   You'll drive me to despair.

Col.   You'll drive me to drink. [*Crosses R. to* Fran.]

Lys.   [c.] [*Aside.*] Give up that superbly beautiful Mayflower
and a million for a California tomboy who carries a gun, whistles
through her teeth, swears in Spanish and rides bareback? Not
while I live! I'll *lie* first. Here goes. [*Aloud.*] Suppose there
is an insurmountable objection to this marriage?

Col.   Surmount it. I'll help you.

Lys.   But if I find it impossible to obey your commands?

Col.   I'd like to see you *disobey*. I make my will to-morrow,
sir.

Lys.   Then uncle, before I explain let me implore your pardon.
[*With assumed dejection going-L. c.*]

Col.   For what? [*Approaching him.*]

Lys.   What I did one year ago at Mount Vernon, Posey county,
Indiana.

Col.   Where votes cost two dollars apiece. Well?

Lys.   I was——

Col.   What? Go on—you were——?

Lys.   [L. c.] Married.

Col.   [c.] Married?

Fran. [R. C.] Married!

Lys. Married.

Col. And without my consent? Oh, you rascal, you villian, you scoundrel—oh, you—you—you—you—you! [*Throws himself gasping with rage on bench.*]

Lys. [C.] I was compelled—forced to marry under cover of a shot gun rammed full of buckshot to the very muzzle. Oh, sir, if you only knew all the circumstances your rage would soon be converted into pity.

Col. [*Changing to helpless grief.*] My boy. My boy this disaster overwhelms your poor old uncle. But come—make a clean breast of the whole bag of tricks.

Lys. My shame and mortification make a confession impossible. Don Francisco will tell you—he knows it all. [*Col. gives way to his grief.*]

Fran. [R. C.] [*Aside.*] I don't know a thing about it.

Lys. [C.] [*Aside.*] That's nothing—Tell him what you *don't* know.

Col. A shot gun wedding!—come Don Francisco—overwhelm a heart broken old uncle with all the disgusting details. Oh, my boy, my boy!

Fran. [*Crosses to him, L.*] I give you my word, sir, this affair has so shocked me that I am as incapable of telling the tale as your own nephew. [*To Lys.*] Come, come, dear friend. Do not weep. Dry your tears. All may yet be well. [*Aside.*] What the deuce am I to say next?

Lys. [C.] [*Aside.*] Anything *anything*. [*Weeps. Goes R.*]

Fran. You see, sir, he is completely unmanned. So am I. [*Weeps.*]

Col. [*Rises.*] Don, you are a sensitive soul. Your kind concern at the misfortunes of my family calls for my most grateful acknowledgment. I will weep with you. [*Weeps on Francisco's shoulder. L. C.*]

Fran. Oh, sir, it is a terrible misfortune.

Col. If you, a stranger, are thus affected, what must an uncle feel?

Fran. More, sir, more—a great sight more!

Col. But we must control ourselves and be men. Let me know the worst at once. Now, sir—at Mount Vernon.———— [*Taking c*]

Fran. [L. C.] Yes—at Mount Vernon.

Col. Posey county, Indiana. [*Looking from one to the other.*]

Fran. Yes, that's right—India county, Posiana.

Lys. Oh, oh, oh—how can I *tell* it? How *can* I tell it!

Col. Oh, Sandy, Sandy—I dread to ask but it must be known. Who is the girl? Tell me, Don. Who is the girl? [*Crosses and flings himself on bench* L.]

Fran. Who is the girl? [*Aside.*] [*Crossing* R.] Whom shall say?

Lys. [R. *Aside.*] Anybody.

Fran. As to the girl, sir, I cannot tell you her name. It wouldn't be right.

Col. Her position in society?

Fran. She's just on the ragged edge. [*Aside.*] Help me out.

Lys. [*Aside.*] Swim out.

Col. I read our disgrace in his reserve—this whispering. Some brazen woman! I'm prepared to hear anything.

Lys. [*Crossing to* C.] It is almost death to me to speak but it would be infamous to let the lady's reputation suffer by my silence. Her character is untarnished.

Col. That's *some* comfort.

Lys. [C.] She is not rich, but well educated.

Col. Her name?

Lys. Martha Mockridge. Her father is mayor of the town. [**Fran.** *crosses* L. *and leans over back of bench.*]

Col. Proceed.

Lys. About a year ago, Derby Dashwood——

Col. The liar?

Lys. Exactly—invested heavily in a gas well at Mount Vernon. I made a trip with him to inspect the purchase, intending to recommend the investment to you should it strike me favorably.

Col. Thoughtful, at least.

Lys. There, at a social gathering, I met the mayor's daughter.

Col. Is she pretty?

Lys. Beautiful as a dream. She *is* a dream.

Col. Skip all that.

Lys. To her beauty she adds culture, refinement and discretion—unless she has forfeited that virtue by fixing her affections on me.

Col. Modestly spoken.

Lys. Dreading her poverty I said nothing to you——

Col. That was wrong, sir.

Lys. And because I feared it might come to your ears I also concealed our love from the lady's family. We met in secret.

Col. [*Sternly reproving.*] Was that deceit, sir? Still - love and prudence, madness and reason. It might be excused.

Lys. One fateful evening the 13th of July, unlucky 13! We were in a retired room innocently exchanging mutual——

Col. You may skip that.

Lys. We thought her father safe at a meeting of the city council, when suddenly he burst in upon us. I had only time to conceal myself in a closet-

Col. Without him seeing you?

Lys. Entirely. But it happened that a cat had a day or two before lodged a family of kittens in the same place. Unluckily I trod upon one of the litter, which so enraged the mother cat that she flew at me with all the fury of a tigress.

Col. I have noticed that the feline species is very fierce in defense of its young. [*Rises.*]

Lys. The noise attracted the old gentleman's attention. He opened the door and dragged me forth.

Col. [*Goes to Lys. and places both hands on his shoulders.*] My boy, my boy—what a situation!

Fran. [L. *Aside.*] I wouldn't accept it at *any* wages.

Lys. [R. C.] I drew my revolver and rushed to the door, but at the top of the stairs———

Col. [c.] Ah ! You were in peril! [*Shaking his head sadly returns to bench and sits.*]

Lys. My foot slipped and I fell head over heels to the bottom. In the fall my revolver was discharged and in an instant her three brothers had rushed upon me from the parlor. urged on by the old man, who encouraged them to murder me, they set upon me most viciously.

Col. They had you completely at their mercy.

Lys. Not quite. With the butt end of my revolver I was giving as good as I got until a big, black, greasy kitchen wench struck my wrist with a heavy poker and disarmed me. The result is obvious. [*Goes R.*]

Col. Marriage became an unavoidable measure in view of the lady's reputation, your condition, her beauty, your love --

Lys. And her father's shot gun loaded to the muzzle.

Col. My boy, you were more unfortunate than culpable.

Lys. [R. *Aside.*] He is relenting. I escape from the California terror and the way is open to my pretty Prudence. If this luck holds up I'll keep my bewitching step-daughter out of the way for a week and—

  Enter **Baby** *and* **Kitty** R. 3 E. Baby *comes down* C.] My dream is shattered. [*Tries to sneak into hotel.*]

Baby. Peek-a-boo! I see you hiding there. [*Drags him down front.*] Tome now—oo Baby wants a tiss. [*Kisses and embraces him.*]

Col. [*Rises excitedly.*] Lysander, who is this female?

Lys. [*Aside to* **Baby** *who is on his* R.] No matter what I say, keep your mouth shut. My life depends on it.

Col. [*Going* C.] Come, sir, I'll stand no further trifling. Who is this woman?

Lys. [C.] Why, sir, she—she is—

Col. [L. C.] Out with it!

Lys. My mother. [**Baby** *screams and faints in Lysander's arms. He passes her to* **Col.** *who makes frantic efforts to pass her back. He dumps her into Francisco's arms, who is at his* L. *elbow and as* **Nell.,** **Derby** *and* **Prud.** *enter from hotel he seizes* **Lys.** *by the collar and forces him to his knees.*]

Derby.
    Prudence,
        Nellie, *all on the steps.*
                Col. *and* **Lys.**   **Baby** *and*
                                        Francisco.
                                        Kitty.

                    Quick Curtain.

ACT II.

[*An hotel parlor. Arch c. Exterior backing. Flat in 3d grooves. Doors* R. *1* E. *and* L. *3.* E. *in box. Large 3-leaf screen just above door* R. *Small stand in* R. *upper corner. Easel with picture between arch and* L. *door. Sofa down* L. *Table with telegraph blanks, paper, pen and ink on it and two chairs down* R. *Carpet down, other chairs, bric-a-brac, etc. At rise* **Col.** *and* **Prudence** *are playing cribbage down* R. *and as curtain goes up* **Nellie** *is finishing a little snatch of song. She is seated on sofa,* L.]

Col. [*After song and looking at cards.*] Very pretty, very pretty indeed.

Nell. I'm glad you like the song, Guardy.

Col. Song? What song? Excuse me, my dear. I wasn't listening. I was alluding to my crib. Fifteen-two, fifteen-four, fifteen-six and six are 12, a pair 14, and a pair 16. [*Pegs game.*] Ah, Miss Prudence, one more hand like that and you will be hopelessly beaten. It's all in the crib, you know.

Prud. Well, it's *my* crib this time and the game isn't lost yet. [*Deals cards.*]

Col. I'm so passionately fond of music. Strange thing that I could never distinguish one tune from another without hearing the words.

Nell. It *is* odd, Guardy. [*Goes up to arch and looks off while* **Prud.** *and* **Col.** *play cards.*]

Col. Was that by Wagner?

Nell. Oh, no—

Col. I thought not. It seems to have some music in it.

Prud. The crib gives me a pair and that just puts me out.

Col. You little witch, you've beaten me after all.

Prud. That pair did it. It's all in the crib you know, sir. Ha, ha!

[*Enter* **Fran.** c.]

Fran. Colonel Lyon. Ladies. [*Bows.*]

Col. Good evening, Don—but it's no use. [*Rises.*] I'll never see that deceitful scamp again.

Nell. [*Going to him* c.] Now Guardy, don't nurse your anger.

Prud. [R.] Please forgive him, sir.

Col. Never! He not only disobeyed me by having anything to do with that woman, but plumped her into my arms as well.

Nell. But she is his mother, sir. Think of his natural affection.

Col. Natural fiddlesticks! I've hated her for thirty years and by the living jingo I shall keep on hating her to the end of the chapter.

Nell. But you shouldn't expect him to hate his mother. It isn't Christianlike.

Col. Persuasion is useless. I'm done with him forever. [*Goes L.*]

Fran. [*Coming down C.*] If you could only see the grief in which my poor friend is plunged

Col. [L.] I don't want to see his grief. He has made his own bed; now let him lie in it.

Fran. [*Aside.*] He'll lie in it, never fear. Even in the grave he'll lie—unless they bury him standing up.

Nell. [R. C.] At least, for my sake, give him a chance to explain.

Col. He *can't* explain.

Fran. [*Aside.*] Oh, *can't* he! He can explain anything.

Prud. [R.] Please hear him, sir.

Col. ' Well I'll see him, but it won't do any good. [*Sits L. on sofa.*]

Fran. Sir, I thank you. Ladies, accept my most respectful gratitude. [*Goes up a little. Aside.*] I've *mixed* those *girls*. When he finds out that he's in love with Nellie, he'll kill me. [*Ex. C.*]

Prud. [R.] I wonder how Dr. Lyon chances to know the general's Brazilian friend?

Nell. [R. C.] Oh, men get acquainted so easily.

Prud. And so do some women.

Nell. What do you mean by that?

Prud. Oh, nothing dear, of course! [*Lys. appears C.*]

Nell. Hush—the general! [*Nell. and Prud. hide behind screen above R. door.*]

Lys. [*Without entering.*] Uncle—speak to me. [*Col. rises.*]

Nell. Uncle! Good heavens, he is Lysander! It is for him we have been pleading.

Prud. Oh, Nell—Isn't it awful! But quick—let us escape. [*Ex. both unseen R. door.*]

Lys. Uncle—have you no word for me?

Col. Yes. You may come in. I thought, sir, that you had something to say to *me*. [*Crosses and sits L. of table.*]

Lys. [*Comes down.*] Only to acknowledge that I disobeyed your most imperative commands in communicating with my mother and to ask your forgiveness.

Col. You knew the result. I make a new will to-morrow, sir.

Lys. [c.] That makes no difference to me, sir.

Col. It doesn't, eh? It makes a difference to you of about $500,000.

Lys. I can bear that, knowing that I have rescued my mother from wretchedness and starvation.

Col. In seeking her out you defied *me.* Nothing can alter that.

Lys. Fate, no act of mine, brought us together. One night, three months ago, while crossing the Strand, I heard a shriek of pain. A woman, faint with hunger, had fallen beneath the horses' feet. With the instinct of the surgeon I forced my way through the crowd and had her taken to Guy's hospital. She was cruelly maimed, and as she lay upon the operating table her eyes opened. "Lysander," she whispered, "my son, my baby. I would have known you among a million by the wart on the side of your nose." [Col. *rises and examins* Lys. *face through his glasses.*] What's the matter, sir?

Col. I'm looking for that infernal wart.

Lys. Next day I had it amputated.

Col. [*Sits down at table.*] What did you bring that woman here for?

Lys. To place her in the home for aged ladies on Staten Island.

Col. That at least was creditable in you, Sandy.

Lys. For myself, I ask nothing, sir. But oh, forgive *her!* Think of her long and bitter repentance—think what a wretch I would be to live on the fat of the land through your abundant generosity while leaving the mother who bore me to die in a ditch.

Col. [*Much moved.*] My boy, my boy—you have a noble heart. [*Rises. Embraces* Lys. *who winks at audience over old man's shoulder.*]

Lys. [*Aside.*] Oh, I couldn't explain a *thing!*

Col. Well, Sandy, I'll go out on the veranda and think it over. [*Ex.* c.]

Lys. He can't lose me. To get out of marrying that California girl I've had to tell a thundering lot of fibs, but the image of Prudence, lovely Prudence, fills my heart and soul. Under the circumstances, what wouldn't a lover do? I'll just go out and help him to think it over. [*Ex.* c.]

Nell. *enters* R. *door.*

Nell. There's nobody here. [**Prud.** *enters* R. *door.*]

Prud. So our general turns out to be Lysander Lyon, a married man and a most unmitigated story teller.

Nell. Yes—but with all due allowance for his awful romance

ing, there's a mystery here that I'd like to see solved. [*Sits* L. *off table.*]

Prud. [c.] There is also a mystery which *I'd* like to solve.

Nell. And that is——?

Prud. Why you are so jealous that this married fabricator has deserted your shrine and commenced worshiping at mine. [*Crosses and sits on sofa.*]

Nell. Don't you take a good deal for granted?

Prud. Haven't I his letter?

Nell. From the way you harp on that absurd note you force me to conclude that you never got one before.

Prud. Don't get angry with *me* dear. *I* didn't spread any net. The bird flew right into the cage without any coaxing whatever.

Nell. What pretty metaphors! You are setting up for a blue-stocking as well as a beauty, I see. The world will confess that your claim to wit at least equals your mortgage on good looks.

Prud. Don't distress yourself about me, dear. The world is not likely to base its judgment on the opinions of a disappointed and envious rival. [*Showing annoyance.*]

Nell. Whatever may be your beauty, Miss Mayflower, your inability to control your temper argues little for your breeding.

Prud. I hope I shall always exhibit a proper resentment at any studied insolence. Our meeting here and its purpose were suggested by you.

Nell. How kind of you to remind me, dear.

Prud. Perhaps you dread the mortification of seeing your boasted fascinations disproved. If so, I shall willingly excuse you from remaining. [*Rises.*]

Nell. [*Rises.*] Oh, indeed! At last the cat is out of the bag! You deliberately provoked a quarrel so that you could receive this married flirt alone. Disingenuous Miss Mayflower! If all Eastern girls are equally innocent I blush for them. [*Goes up.*]

Prud. If all Western girls resemble you, Miss Goldengate, they have my sincere pity.

Nell. [*Turns up* c.] We Western girls are better brought up than to brazenly acknowledge an infatuation for a married man.

Prud. Then I suppose our plan is abandoned?

Nell. [*Comes down a little* c.] I am ready to carry it out on one condition.

Prud. Name it.

Nell. That you allow me to assume your name throughout the interview.

Prud. Oh, certainly! Any little thing like that, dear, of course. [*Sarcastically. Sits* L.]

Nell. Pray save your sarcasm until after the test. Hark! I hear footsteps. [*Runs. up and looks off c.*] It is Dr. Lyon. Don't let him see you. [*Comes down c.*].

Prud. [*Crossing R.*] Have no fear that I shall bungle my part, Miss Goldengate. [*Hides below screen.*]

Enter **Lysander.**]

Lys. Fortune favors me. She is alone. Miss Mayflower. Am I right? [*Up c.*]

Nell. [*Down beside table.*] I see, sir, that you have received my letter.

Lys. And flew to keep the appointment with———[*Coming down eagerly.*]

Nell. No nonsense, please. Don't think that this meeting was meant to encourage you.

Lys. I was hardly so presumptuous. [**Prud.** *slips around between screen when he has passed.*]

Nell. [*R.C.*] The fact is that your conversation was so very interesting this morning—

Lys. [*Down c.*] Thanks. [*Aside.*] That's my long suit and the only way I can dodge the sharp questioning of little Tootsywootsy. [*Going L.*]

Prud. [*Peeping from behind screen. Aside.*] When did I ever converse with him?

Nell. [*Aside.*] You saw him this morning.

Prud. [*Aside.*] Yes—but the conversation was with you.

Nell. [*Aside.*] Exactly, dear. Some people are *so* obtuse! [**Prud.** *disappears.*]

Lys. [*L.*] I hope, then, that we shall become very much better acquainted.

Nell. You are already better known than you imagine.

Lys. [*Aside.*] I hope not!

Nell. Your name is Lyon.

Lys. [*Aside!*] The deuce! [*Aloud*] True—Lysander Lyon, M. D.

Nell. When do you return to Brazil, general?

Lys. Ha, ha, ha! Really, Miss Mayflower, I must apologize for that outrageous Brazilian story. I certainly thought you knew I was joking.

Nell. Oh, that was merely a *joke*.

Lys. That's all, upon my honor, and I hope you will forgive it I have heard it remarked that my jokes are apt to be taken somewhat seriously. [*He sits on sofa.*]

Nell. Have you ever heard of a Miss Goldengate? [*Sitting L. of table.*]

Lys. Frequently.

Nell. Have you ever had any serious intentions regarding her? [*Aside to* **Prud.** *who is peeping.*] Listen, dear.

Lys. If you mean as a lover, never! But the lady, I believe, does me the honor to have quite serious designs on me.

Prud. [*Aside.*] I hear every word, dear. [*Maliciously.*]

Nell. I have been told, however --

Lys. By the lady herself? She has a most fertile imagination.

Prud. [*Aside.*] I'm listening, dear.

Nell. I have been told that you know something about a lady at Mount Vernon, Indiana.

Lys. By Miss Goldengate—just as I surmised. Well, I do know all there is to know about that lady.

Nell. [*Rising indignantly.*] That being the case, sir, how dare you, a married man, insult me by offering your odious attentions?

Lys. The Hoosier lady, I assure you, would not object. [*Smiling. Remains seated.*]

Nell. Would not object?

Lys. Not in the least. The only wife I have is in my mind.

Nell. In your mind!

Lys. Just so. A mere creature of the imagination. The attacks of the Goldengate girl were so powerfully backed by my uncle's positive commands that to protect myself from her I invented the Hoosier lady, marriage and all. I'm only surprised that I didn't invent a family also on the spur of the moment.

Nell. Granting that your defense is true, was your action honorable? [*Sits* R. *of table.*]

Lys. [*Rises and crosses* R.] Miss Mayflower should be the last to condemn me for a moral lapse her own charms have occasioned. No other motive than the fear of losing you could have prevailed on me to deceive my uncle and infringe those laws which I have hitherto inviolably observed.

Nell. What laws, sir?

Lys. The sacred laws of truth! [*Sits* R. *of table.*]

Nell. Poor Miss Goldengate!

Lys. Are you acquainted with her?

Nell. I have heard of her; but you, I presume, have been long on an intimate footing?

Lys. We were raised together.

Nell. [*Aside.*] Again in his mind. [*Aloud.*] Is she handsome?

Lys. Her paint comes from Paris and her maid is quite an artist.

Nell. Her form?

Lys. Thanks to the corset maker and her ladies' tailor, quite a work of art.

Nell. Her style?

Lys. Wildly Western—uses slang, carries a gun, whistles through her teeth, swears in Spanish and thinks nothing of breaking a bucking broncho before breakfast.

Nell. What a graphic picture! How about her intellect?

Lys. To do her justice, naturally bright but uncultivated.

Nell. Education?

Lys. Neglected.

Nell. Taste?

Lys. Atrocious.

Nell. Temper?

Lys. Vile.

Nell. Delightful creature! But come, these are not your real opinions. You think it will flatter me to belittle the charms of your uncle's ward.

Lys. If you do not think me commonly candid at least give me credit for the courage of my convictions.

Nell. Would you dare to acknowledge them before the lady's face?

Lys. At the first opportunity.

Nell. Will you meet her here?

Lys. When?

Nell. In half an hour.

Lys. The sooner the better.

Nell. Then in half an hour. [*Rises.*] Be punctual. [*Crosses to* c.]

Lys. [*Rises.*] I shall be here. [*Crosses up* L.] Till then, au revoir. [*Ex.* L. *door.* **Prud.** *slips between screen and box as he passes.*]

Prud. [*Down* R.] You don't know how sorry I felt for you, dear.

Nell. [c.] Before I am through with him *he* will be the person to be pitied. But come, we both want revenge—let us plan it. [*Ex. door* R.]

Derb. [*Without.*] Now really, dear girls—I can't do it, you know—I have a dreadful cold really. [*Enters* c.] It's a dreadful thing to be so awfully popular. [*Comes down.*] Now, where the deuce is the Colonel?

[**Col.** *enters* c.]

Derb. Ah, Colonel—you were looking for me?

Col. Yes sir, I was. [*Coming down.*] I am informed that you own a gas well at Mount Vernon, Indiana.

Derb. [L. C.] Then your informant lied abominniably, don't you know. [*Sits on sofa.*]

Col. [*Aside.*] More lies—more deception. I'll disinherit him. [*Sits L. of table.*]

Derb. The only thing I own in that town is a hole in the ground that was once *suspected* of being a gas well.

Col. [*Aside.*] Then it was *not* deception, after all. [*Aloud.*] Do you know the Mayor of Mount Vernon?

Derb. Oh, yes—Mayor Perkins.

Col. No sir—Mayor Mockridge.

Derb. Mount Vernon is my home, don't you know, and there never has been any mayor of that name.

Col. [*Aside.*] Lysander's description fits him to a hair. He's a *liar.* [*Aloud.*] Your pretended ignorance of the Mockridge family is a generous but unnecessary proof of your friendship for my nephew. But I know all about it.

Derb. About what?

Col. Lysander's marriage.

Derb. What Lysander?

Col. Why, my nephew, Lysander.

Derb. Is *he married?* [*Starting to his feet.*]

Col. [*Rising.*] Is he *married?* You *know* he is!

Derb. Do I? Well, if I do I didn't know I did

Col. See here, Dashwood, this thing has gone far enough. He has confessed it himself.

Derb. He has? Really!

Col. [C.] Yes, sir, to *me.* Every circumstance—going with you to Mount Vernon to inspect your gas well—meeting Martha, the mayor's daughter, at a party—stolen interviews—surprised by the father—kittens—pistol—poker—shot gun and marriage. Not a detail lacking.

Derb. [L. C.] And this account was given you by your nephew?

Col. By Lysander himself this afternoon. What had I better do?

Derb. Kill him—I mean, accept my congratulations. [*Holds out hand.*]

Col There is little reason for congratulation, sir.

Derb. Oh—I see—you don't approve of the match.

Col. Not while I'm awake.

Derb. Well, don't lose any sleep over it.

Col. What do you mean, sir?

Derb. That you have one of the most desirable nieces by marriage in the whole United States.

Col. So you *do* know her. I thought we'd get at the truth after a little. [*Aside. Returning to chair* R. C.] They can't fool me. I know when a man is lying in a minute.

Derb. [C.] She may not have brought Lysander a fortune, but she'll never cost him a dollar.

Col. Just what he says. [*Sitting chair* L. *of table.*]

Derb. And you needn't make any provision in your will for her children.

Col. Why not? You mean—

Derb. She hasn't any.

Col. Ha, ha, ha.

Derb. Ha, ha, ha! [*Throws himself on the sofa in a paroxysm of laughter.*]

Col. Something seems to tickle you, sir.

Derb. This is too rich—ha, ha, ha! it is, by Jove!

Col. Sir! [*Rising.*]

Derb. I beg your pardon—really—but this marriage—ha, ha, ha!

Col. Well, sir? [*Annoyed.*]

Derb. Never took place.

Col. [*Going* C.] Absurd! Do you suppose my nephew would dare to impose upon me, sir?

Derb. He'd dare to impose upon anybody, he would, by Jove! I know him.

Col. What do you know of him?

Derb. That he is the most irrepressible falsifier I ever met; and that whether from constitution or habit, there's no believing a word he says.

Col. Very shrewd, sir, to attempt to turn the tables on Lysander, but your own reputation for unveracity has preceeded you, and by the living jingo, sir, I'm too old a chicken to be fooled by a hen. [*Throws himself angrily into chair* L. *of table.*]

Derb. Sir! [*Rising with indignation.*]

Col. My nephew's character can't be blasted by the breath of a notorious bouncer.

Derb. Bouncer? What the dickens do you mean, sir? [*Crossing* R. *and blustering.*]

Col. [*Inraged.*] I said "bouncer" for the sake of euphony, sir. [*Rises.*] But if you prefer the old fashioned Saxon word "liar" you may have it, sir, and be d—d to you.

Derb. [C.] You're an old bully.

Col. You're a young Joe Mulhatton.

Derb. [c.] If your outrageous conduct wasn't inspired by some of your nephew's infernal lies, even your age wouldn't protect you, sir. No, by Jove! [*Goes up a little.*]

Col. [*Squaring off at him and dancing around, whooping mad.*] Don't let my age or anything worry you. Sail right in you little shrimp. Sail in and let me show you something scientific. [*Nell. enters R. door.*]

Nell. [R. c. *in front of table.*] Guardy—Mr. Dashwood—what does this mean?

Derb. [L.] Aw—aw -the Colonel is just showing me how the houla-houla ladies from Honolulu used to trip it on the Midway, don't you know.

Nell. [*Horrified.*] The houla-houla! Oh, Colonel—shame!

Col. [c.] I'll punch your head when I get you outside. If I don't, sir, damme!

Derb. Don't wait till you get outside, old chappie.

Nell. [*Crossing* L.] Mr. Dashwood, you've been in a quarrelsome mood all day. Now I insist upon knowing what this is all about.

Col. [*Dropping down to table.*] Young puppy—he had the gall to contradict me and attempted to brand my nephew as a falsifier. I repeat it, sir, Lysander *is* married.

Derb. [L. c.] To an imaginary woman. And because I refused to acknowledge knowing this lady's family you took to carrying on like John L. Sullivan on a rampage. [*Turning to Nell.*] Wanted to fight me, by Jove. But I spared him, don't you know.

Nell. [*To* Col. *crossing to* c.] I'm sorry to take sides against you, dear, but

Col. My dear! [**Derb.** *drops down and sits on sofa.*]

Nell. Lysander has just corroborated Mr. Dashwood.

Col. He *isn't* married? It's all a falsehood?

Nell. Precisely. But the excuses he gives for his extraordinary fibs are as singular as the story itself.

Col. What are they?

Nell. An unconquerable aversion to me, whom he has seen but once, and a wild infatuation for Prudence, whom I am almost sure he never saw in his life.

Col. The unblushing scamp! You know how I have forgiven his faults, condoned his extravagance and all? Well, I'll do no more of it. I hereby call myself out and go on a strike [*Sits.*]

Nell. [R. c.] Oh, don't say that, sir.

Col. I repeat it—I forever cast him off as a graceless, abandoned, ungrateful, heartless young spendthrift—

Nell. Tut, tut, tut! [*Puts hand over his mouth and whispers to him.*]

Col. Eh? What? [*She whispers and he grins.*] Ho, ho, ho! Oh, well—that's a horse of another color.

Nell. Under the circumstances will you let me undertake his reformation? I think I can both punish him and effect a cure.

Col. Well—well—Puss—you may try it.

Nell. He will return in a minute and you must draw from him the truth of the Mount Vernon business. You must also consent to his marrying Prudie.

Col. But I don't want him to marry Prudie. If he does, he'll contract the chewing gum habit and I hate it.

Nell. [*Goes c.*] Don't be alarmed—he'll never marry her. Your arm, Mr. Dashwood.

Derb. [*Crossing to c. hurriedly.*] But he ought to apologize, don't you know. I insist—really.

Nell. [*Pulling him R.*] Oh nonsense—he's an old gentleman and you ought to have more sense.

Derb. Should I, really? By Jove!

[*Ex. with Nell. R. door.*]

Col. [*Looking after them. Rises.*] That young sprig will never be satisfied till I give him a lesson in scrapping.

[*Lysander enters c.*]

Lys. What—Uncle Dick still here? This is my time for disappearing. [*Going c.*]

Col. Stop, sir! I want you. What brings you here again?

Lys. I thought it my duty, sir, to call on Miss Goldengate and make some suitable apology for my unfortunate conduct—and—and—you understand. [*Coming down.*]

Col. Um! You wanted to square yourself, eh? Very polite, sir. Devilish polite!

Lys. I'm glad my conduct meets with your approval. [*Sits on sofa L.*]

Col. [*E. C. Aside with suppressed rage.*] Oh, it does—it *does!* *Aloud.*] Now, sir, I've been thinking about that poor girl in Indiana. As things have turned out it isn't decent to leave her with her own people any longer.

Lys. [*Alarmed.*] Sir! [*Jumps up.*]

Col. I'll wire her. [*Sits and write telegram.*]

Lys. [*L. Aside.*] He'll wire her because I've been stringing him. If he telegraphs to Mount Vernon the message will be returned in a few hours and he'll catch onto the fake.

Col. There. That'll do. [*Reads.*] "All is forgiven. Am anxious to greet my niece. Catch first train and join Lysander here. Wire me when you leave. Uncle Dick." I'll just step into the office and file it. [*Rising to go up.*]

Lys. [*Aside.*] The dickens he will! [*Stops him.*] You mustn't send that!

Col. Why not?

Lys. Because she wouldn't dare to undertake the journey at present.

Col. Why not? What's the matter with her?

Lys. [L. C.] Why, uncle, she's an invalid.

Col. [C.] Eh, what? Oh you don't say. [*Aside.*] This caps the climax!

Lys. A journey of 1,000 miles just now would be madness.

Col. Not at all, sir. She can have a Pullman state room all to herself and there won't be the slightest danger.

Lys. Impossible! Her father, the mayor, depends on the labor vote for re-election, and if his daughter should patronize the Pullman company, the unions would boycott him as sure as fate.

Col. I'll write, then, and ask him about that. [*Goes to table.*]

Lys. [C.] Do, sir. The old gentleman would be delighted to receive a letter from you—I have sung your praises to him so often.

Col. [*Aside.*] The scamp is positively cross eyed in moral obliquity. [*Aloud.*] That was kind in you. I'll write. Let me see—how do you address him? [*About to sit.*]

Lys. I always say, "Dear Father-in-law."

Col. No, no—his postoffice address.

Lys. Why, Mount Vernon, Posey county, Indiana. But you needn't trouble. I shall write my wife by this mail and I'll enclose your letter to her father.

Col. [*Aside.*] He's like a weasel. I can't catch him asleep. [*Aloud.*] That'll do first rate. [*Sits down. Dips pen in ink.*]

Lys. [*Aside.*] Mighty short curves but I took them all. Talk about shooting the chutes! [*Sits on sofa.*]

Col. On second thought, Sandy, that would look rather too familiar.

Lys. Why so?

Col. Oh, officials in small towns feel their oats a good deal and have a very keen sense of their dignity. Give me his address and I'll mail my own letter.

Lys. Why, I just gave it to you.

Col. Yes—but his name. I've been so upset that I've completely forgotten it.

Lys. [*Aside.*] Confound it! So have I! [*Aloud.*] His name? What, you've forgotten it already? Ha, ha, ha!

Col. I have. [*Dryly.*]

Lys. Why, his name is Hopkinson.

Col. Hopkinson? Did you say *Hopkinson?* [*Aside.*] I've got him at last! [*Gleefully.*]

Lys. Yes, sir. H-o-p-k-i-n-s-o-n.

Col. That isn't the name you gave me before, sir. [*Severely.*]

Lys. Ha, ha, ha! I beg your pardon, sir. Ha, ha, ha! [*Aside.*] What the deuce name *did* I give him? Ha, ha, ha! [*Very forced laugh.*]

Col. What are you laughing at?

Lys. At your not allowing me to know the name of my own father-in-law.

Col. I can't help it, sir. That wasn't the name you gave me before. It sounded more like monkey wrench—or mockery—or mock—mock something.

Lys. Oh—Mockridge—of course—the Honorable *Hopkinson* Mockridge. I thought you asked for his *given* name.

Col. [*Rises.*] You are the champion, sir; but enough of this. Miss Mayflower has told me of your confession that Martha Mockridge is a myth.

Lys. [*Rises. Aside.*] Here comes that silver dollar to buy a rope!

Col. [*Goes* c.] How dare you call yourself a gentleman—you whose life has been one continual scene of fraud and falsity? You, who have not spared me, your benefactor, from your infamous deceptions? [*Both hands in pants pockets, legs spread apart, facing* Lys.]

Lys. Hear me, sir, I entreat—

Col. To be again imposed upon? No sir—my eyes are opened at last. [*Goes a little* R.]

Lys. [*Following him, appealingly.*] By all that's sacred, sir!

Col. [R. C.] I'm deaf to your fictions from this time on.

Lys. [C.] This is the truth. The Mount Vernon affair is all a fable.

Col. And how *dare* you—

Lys. Just one minute. Before you insisted upon my courting Miss Goldengate, I met a lady—

Col. Stop! Stop! Another trumped up woman and fabulous wedding. [*Putting hands over ears and going up. Turns.*] Do you take me for a fool?

Lys. This lady is not trumped up nor has the marriage taken place.

Col. Her name?

Lys. Prudence Mayflower and I love her to distraction. [*Goes* L. C.]

Col. What right have you to love anybody without my consent? Besides, she chews gum.

Lys. [*Turning.*] Well, I choose her.

Col. Have you spoken to her? [*Comes down* c.]

Lys. I only parted with her ten minutes ago and returned by her invitation.

Col. You won't stick to her.

Lys. I will, like mucilage.

Col. Very well, sir. I'm an old friend of the Mayflower family and I'll investigate this latest shift in the cut; but if I catch you in the smallest falsehood or the least duplicity I'm done with you forever. [*Goes* R.]

Lys. I should deserve nothing better.

Col. Wait for me here.

Lys. I have one other confession to make.

Col. What—more deception? [*Returning a few steps.*]

Lys. [R. C.] No—only suppression. I intend to make a clean breast of everything, ask your forgiveness and stick to the truth, the whole truth, and nothing but the truth, so help me Bob, forever more, amen. [*Raising* R. *hand.*]

Col. [C. *Aside.*] Hell is paved with good intentions. [*Aloud.*] Out with it!

Lys. Six months ago I married a widow with $250,000.

Col. [*Going* R. *with hands over ears.*] Enough! Enough! [*Turns.*] You need a *keeper!*

Lys. This is the solemn, bitter truth. From the bottom of my heart I wish it was only a bad dream. She concealed the fact that she had an incumbrance until after our marriage, and when she died, two months later, I found that the entire property reverted to my step-daughter.

Col. Then you are a widower? [*Suspiciously.*]

Lys. [C.] Thank heaven, I am! [*Piously.*]

Col. Encumbered with a step-daughter? [*With horror.*]

Lys. Heaven help me, yes. [*Despairingly.*]

Col. That settles you with Prudence. I've heard her say a hundred times that she wouldn't marry a widower for a million, or a widower with a child for half the earth.

Lys. My poor innocent child! I give you my sacred word, sir, that if you will use your influence to overcome Miss Mayflower's objections I will never again do a single thing to grieve you.

Col. [*Goes* C.] That's a bargain. I'll give you one more chance, and one only.

Lys. Uncle Dick, you are the most generous man on earth. [*Holding out hand and* **Col.** *offers pocket book.*]

Col. I'm not doing this for your sake, but because Prudence *may* have had the bad taste to fall in love with you. I'll go and see. [*Ex.* R. *door.*]

Lys. Every obstacle is removed but one—my precious step-child. I'll ship her to Australia or send her to Japan as a missionary in the morning. Anything to prevent her bobbing up again to ruin everything.

[*Enter* **Baby** c.]

Baby. Papa.

Lys. My hideous fate pursues me still! [*Throws himself on lounge.*]

Baby. [*Coming down* c.] I've been searching for you everywhere, papa. Look at that. [*Opens package.*] Thirteen cigar butts. It's an outrage.

Lys. Go home.

Baby. I shan't go home to a balcony all strewn with filthy, nasty, reeking cigar stumps. It's disgusting!

Lys. How dare you dog my footsteps? Cigar stumps! Bosh! You've been spying.

Baby. [c.] Yes, I *have*, and I've found out your little game. You want to put another woman in the place of my dear mama, but you shan't do it. No, sir! You don't marry again until I'm provided with a husband. [*Goes up a little.*]

Lys. [*Rises and points* c.] Go home, Miss. I command you.

Baby. [*Turning*] Command *me!* I like your nerve. [*Comes down* c.]

Lys. What do you mean to do?

Baby. Introduce myself to my new mama as her little daughter.

Lys. Go home! [*In stern command, pointing* c.]

Baby. I shan't! This is a public parlor and I have as much right here as you have.

Lys. [*Aside.*] I've got to square her. [*Aloud*] My love, do you really want a husband?

Baby. Do I really want a husband! Have I done a thing except chase men and try to capture one in the last thirty years?

Lys. What kind of a husband would you prefer, my love?

Baby. [*Goes bashfully* R. *and sits* L. *of table.*] Well, papa, my taste has always run toward a nice, meek little husband—one I could train to obey my every whim and all that sort of thing. But, of course, under the circumstances I can't afford to be any too particular.

Lys. [c.] You can't, indeed! With your future waltzing away off into your past at the rate of 365 and a quarter days every year, you haven't time!

Baby. You are trying to insult me but thank heaven I inherited a sweetly serene temper from my own dear papa.

Lys. If that's where you got it, I'm glad I never had to live with the old gentleman. [*Goes a little* L.] Now listen. I'll make a contract with you. If you'll go home immediately and keep the fact that you are my daughter discreetly hidden until I give you leave to reveal it, I'll get you a husband.

Baby. A real, nice, meek, little husband, papa?

Lys. If one of that brand is to be had. At any rate a suitable husband.

Baby. How soon?

Lys. Within a month.

Baby. That's wasting time. Within a week.

Lys. [*Aside.*] I'm desperate. [*Aloud.*] I'll do it.

Baby. [*Rises.*] It's a contract. But if you break your word, papa dear, you know me.

Lys. Oh yes— I know you my angel child—good night. [*Waring her up* C.]

Baby. Kiss me good night, papa. [*Goes to him mincingly, holding up her face.*]

Lys. [*Kisses her.*] Good night--oh, get out. [*Turning away in disgust.*]

Baby. [C.] Get a move on yourself, papa, for you've got to hustle this week. Ha, ha, ha! [*Ex.* C.]

Lys. Reason begins to totter upon her throne. Let her tot. Ha, ha, ha! I'm going mad—mad—mad! Find a husband for *her* within a week? Nobody but a madman would attempt it!

[Enter Col. R. door.]

Col. Well, sir, much to my surprise, I find that you have told the truth at last and that Prudence will accept you in spite of your incumbrance.

Lys. [C.] She will! Say - let's call a preacher and get married to-night.

Col. [R. C.] Don't talk foolishness. She has so far revised her former opinions that she is prepared to love your little Tootsy-wootsy for your sake.

Lys. She will, she *will!* She couldn't *help* loving her!

Col. [*Opening* R. *door.*] Come Prudence. Your luck is something phenomenal, sir.

[Enter Prud. R. door.]

Lys. [*Seeing* **Prud.** *With a groan.*] It is! [*Falls back* L.]

Col. [*Leading* **Prud.** C. *to* **Lys.**] If he is not sensible of the favor you do him in accepting a widower with an encumbrance I'll disown him. There, my boy, take her and make her happy.

Lys. [L.] Take her? [*Aside.*] I'll take castor oil first.

Col. She is more than you deserve, I know, but let your future good behavior testify your gratitude.

Lys. Uncle—I—I—

Col. [R. C.] Now, then, don't stand there like a petrified puppy—make your acknowledgments to the lady.

Lys. To *that* lady?

Col. To be sure—to Miss Prudence Mayflower.

Lys. That lady Miss Mayflower?

Col. No more trifling, sir. Recollect that I make my will to-morrow. Take her hand this minute or suffer the consequences.

Lys. [L. *Aside.*] Just as I feared. I *have* become insane and this is one of my delusions. [*Takes her hand as* **Fran.** *enters C. and* **Nell.** *enters R. door disguised.*]

Col. [C. *and behind them.*] Bless you, my children.

Nell. [*Down* R. C. *Accusingly in tragic tones.*] False, per-jured wretch! Thank heaven I have arrived in time to prevent you from blasting another life. Monster! [*Crosses L.*]

Lys. What do you mean? [**Prud.** *goes* R.]

Nell. Cruel, cruel man! But we shall never part again. [*Clinging to him.*]

Lys. [L. C.] The deuce we shan't! [*Repulsing her.* **Fran.** *drops down* R. *corner.*]

Nell. [L.] Not one kind look, not one tender word to greet me? Oh this is cruel, cruel! [*Down to* L. *corner.*]

Lys. What the deuce *is* all this? Are *you* mad? Am *I* mad? Are we *all* mad? Is this a lunatic asylum?

Nell. This is my reward for weary months of suffering and sorrow—you pretend you do not even *know* the woman whom you swore at the altar to love, cherish and protect!

Col. [C.] Madame, you seem to know this gentleman.

Nell. Only too well!

Col. His name?

Nell. Lysander Lyon.

Col. And yours?

Nell. Martha Lyon, his lawful wife.

Lys. [L. C.] Uncle, so help me—[*Puts up right hand.*]

Col. [C. *Pulls down his hand*] Don't perjure yourself, sir! One question more—your maiden name?

Nell. Mockridge—Martha Mockridge.

Col. Of Posey county, Indiana?

Nell. Yes sir.

Col. Wretch!

Lys. I swear by all that's—

Col. Measureless, boundless, endless liar!

Lys. You refuse to listen to me—at least hear Don Francisco.

Fran. [R. *corner.*] No you don't. You can't drag me into your scrape. I'm no Brazilian nobleman and you know it. You hired me in New York three days ago and I'm your valet.

Omnes. His valet!

Prud. [R.] Deceiver!

Nell. [L.] Impostor!

Col. [R. C.] Liar!

Lys. [*Taking* c.] I *will* be heard! No matter what romancing I may have been guilty of in the past, this woman is not my wife. The only wife I ever had has been dead four months and I helped to plant her. As for you, I don't know whether you are Miss Mayflower or not, but I solemnly declare that until my uncle forced me to betroth myself to you I never set eyes on you in all my life.

Col. Didn't I plead with her at your own request? [*Pointing at* Lys.]

Lys. No!

Prud. [R.] Didn't you write a letter? [*Pointing finger at* Lys.

Lys. [c.] No!

Nell. [L.] Am not I your wife? [*Pointing finger at* Lys.

Lys. No!

Fran. [L.] Didn't you instruct me to back up your lies? [*Pointing finger at* Lys.]

Col. [R. C.] Didn't you tell me the story of your marriage? [*Pointing finger at* Lys.

Lys. Yes—no—no! [*All continue pointing.*]

Nell. Listen to me. [*Slapping hands together. All stop pointing.*]

Lys. No!

Col. Haven't I—[*Slapping hands together.*]

Lys. No! No! No! No! *You're* crazy, *she's* crazy, you're *all* crazy, and if I stop here another minute I'll catch the infection. [*Rushes to door* R. **Derb.** *enters and stops him.*]

Derb. No you don't, by Jove! [**Lys.** *rushes across* L. *but* **Nell.** *stops him.*]

Nell. [*Taking off hat and veil.*] Ha, ha, ha!

Omnes. Ha, ha, ha! [**Baby** *and* **Kitty** *appear* c. *for tableau.*]

Lys. Miss Mayflower!

Nell. [*Crossing to* c.] No—Miss Goldengate—the California terror who whistles through her teeth, carries a gun and swears in Spanish—all at your service. [*Curtseys.*]

Baby, Kitty.

Derby.

Colonel.

Prudence,

Nellie.

Francisco.

Lysander.

Curtain.

[*Distribution of characters at end of act.*]

-

ACT III.

[*Sitting room at Arlington Villa. Arch c. Flat in 3d Grooves Doors* L. 1 E., L. 2 F., R. 2 E. *in box. Balustrade back of arch and sea horizon backing. Table with newspaper on it and two chairs down* L. C. *Sofa* R. *Sideboard across* L. *upper corner with decanter, water, glasses, etc. Chairs* R. *and* L. *of arch. Small stand* R. *against box. Chair* L. *against box. Carpet down; rugs, bric-a-brac, etc. At rise* Kitty *with broom and* Fran. *in livery disc. up stage beside arch.*]

Kitty. Well, did you ever, Francisco? I don't do a thing all day but sweep off the cigar stumps thrown down by that little dude up stairs.

Fran. He's no man at all or he'd show himself when *I'm* around.

Kitty. Look, will you—three—five—ten—fourteen cigar ends. [*Shows them in dust pan.*] I like work. I'm much obliged to him. [*Looks up and calls.*] I like cleaning up other peoples' dirt, I don't think.

Baby. [*Without; calling.*] Fran—cis—co!

Fran. There she is—confound her. [*Calling.*] Yes, Miss—coming. [*Kisses* Kitty. *Ex.* R. Kitty *squeals.*]

Lys. [*Entering door* R.] What the deuce is all this noise? What are you squealing about, Kitty? I want you to put an end to it at once.

Kitty. I don't have to put an end to it. There are fourteen ends to it already and it isn't ten o'clock yet. Look! [*Shows stumps.*]

Lys. Who the deuce *is* the fellow? What does he look like?

Kitty. He's a little, sawed-off, pushed down imitation of a man and dresses like a dude.

Lys. I'll fix him. I'll punch his head. [*Goes on balcony and calls.*] Hello, you! Hello there! Johnny Smoker—hello!

Derb. [*Above and out of sight.*] Do you take me for a telephone? What do you mean by hello?

Lys. What do I mean by hello! He's an idiot! I'll tell you what I mean, sir. You have a disgusting habit of throwing your snipes on my balcony.

Derb. And why shouldn't I?

Lys. Because it's a filthy habit and I don't like it. Can't you throw them into the street?

Derb. And have them fall on people's heads? Not much! It's against the ordinances, don't you know.

Lys. You don't seem to care whether they fall on *my* head or not.

Derb. Oh, there's nothing in *that*, don't you know!

Lys. There isn't, eh? My head's as good as yours. I'd like to feel your bumps for about a minute—and let you feel mine. [*Strikes pugilistic attitude.*] Why don't you show yourself? [*Looking up.*]

Derb. Oh, go to bed. You're dreaming.

Lys. You're a *nice* young man! I'd like to meet you—in a quiet, retired spot, all alone. [*Reenters through arch.*]

Derb. Oh—have a smoke! [*Lighted cigar stump falls on balcony.*]

Kitty. That's fifteen! [*Picks it up.*]

Lys. I'll put a stop to this business. Pick up all those snipes, Kitty, and wrap them in paper. [*Calls.*] Hello, you, up there. [*Going out.*] I'm going straight to the police station with your filthy snipes and my hired girl as witnesses.

Derb. Oh, go to thunder!

Lys. He's an anarchist. He isn't afraid of the law. [*Reenters room.*]

Kitty. [*Looks up.*] Here he is—quick.

Lys. [*Rushing out.*] I'll have the law on him!

Kitty. Too late—he's gone again.

Lys. That shows he's an anarchist—he's so scared of the law. You needn't mind those snipes, Kitty—throw them out. I've changed my mind. [*Comes down* c.]

Kitty. [*Aside.*] Barking dogs never bite. [*Ex.* R. U. E.]

Lys. [*Sits down and picks up paper.*] I wonder whether they put in that paragraph I sent them? Yes—here it is. [*Reads.*] "It is rumored that Dr. Lysander Lyon, nephew of Col. Lyon, the California millionaire, is soon to wed Miss Nellie Goldengate of San Francisco. The bride elect is one of the wealthiest heiresses of Newport's season." Pleasant news for Dashwood, poor devil. He has lost his government job and hasn't a cent. [*Bells rings off* L.] Hello! there's the bell and Kitty has gone to throw out those confounded snipes. [*Opens door* L. 1 E. *Enter* Col. *and* Nell.]

Col. Aha, my boy, we've found you at last.

Lys. [*Aside.*] Oh, Lord I thought I was safe! [*Aloud.*] Sit down here, dear. Uncle, you are old enough to find a chair for yourself. [*Conducting* Nell. *to sofa.*]

Nell. What a pretty view you have of the sea.

Col. Very pleasant quarters—for a bachelor on $1000 a year. I don't see how he does it. [*Sits in arm chair* R. *of table.*]

Lys. [R. C. *Aside.*] If Baby comes back before they go I'm done for! [*All through the scene he is nervously watching doors* L, 1E. *and* C.] You are out early, uncle.

Col. Yes. I had a bad night. You know how sick I was yesterday?

Lys. Indeed, no! [*Crosses* L. *and sits beside table.*]

Col. Yes you do—that feeling of fullness after eating—all down here and—

Lys. Yes, yes—so much the better. [*Aside.*] Where the thunder is Kitty?

Col. So much the better?

Lys. No, no—I said you are so much better.

Col. On the contrary, I am much worse.

Lys. Then so much the worse. [*Aside.*] If I could only give Kitty a tip to warn her off!

Col. This thing is serious. Every time I eat, and indeed, I may say even when I don't eat, I feel a sort of a, kind of a all down here, and then all through there—a kind of a—

Lys. What?

Col. That's the point—what? I don't know, Nell doesn't know, and no more does Dr. Briggs.

Lys. Well, I'll take my oath *I* don't.

Col. We are on our way to the specialist's office and thought
we'd pop in on you to have a look at the baby. Nell is just dy-
ing to see the dear little Tootsywootsey.

Lys. [*Aside.*] She'll fall dead when she *does.*

Nell. I fairly dote on children, especially little girls.

Lys. So do I!

Nell. Where is the little pet? Can we see her?

Lys. Not for the world! She's having her morning nap.

Col. I say, Sandy—is she—is she weaned? [**Nell.** *very much
embarrassed*]

Lys. [*Aside.*] Rather— about the year 1847! [*Aloud.*] Oh,
yes—she's weaned—very nearly.

Nell. Has she any teeth?

Lys Yes, she has *some* teeth. [*Aside.*] On a gold plate.

Nell. How many?

Lys. Eighteen hundred and forty-seven.

Nell. What!

Lys. No—no—I was thinking of something else.

Col. *I* was just thinking, she must have got about all of them.

Nell. How absurd! Ha, ha! Now I'm to have the first kiss
when she wakes up.

Lys. Of course you shall, dear. [*Aside.*] And I hope you'll
enjoy it!

Nell. I've brought her the cutest little hood, all trimmed with
lace. See! [*Shows it.*]

Lys. Lovely! She'll look like an angel in it!

Col. And I've brought her a jumping jack—such a gay-
colored fellow, to be her little husband. [*Shows parcel. Puts
back in pocket.*]

Lys. The very thing. She'll be delighted with a little husband. [*Aside.*] Even if he *is* a gay colored fellow.

Col You don't think the toy is too old for her?

Lys. Oh, you don't need to be afraid of *that*. [*Aside.*] Too
old for *her!*

Col. [*Rises.*] But come, Sandy; where is all your politeness?
I'm getting hungry and we'd like to wash our hands before lunch,
you know.

Lys. [*Rises.*] How thoughtless of me! Nellie, would you
mind using this room? [*Hands her to door* L. *Aside.*] Where
the dickens is Kitty? Gossiping with the other servant girls, I
suppose.

Nell. [*At door* L. 2 E.] Now mind you let me know the very
moment dear little Tootsywootsey wakens.

Lys. Oh, of course. I only hope you'll be as pleased with her as you anticipate. [*Ex. with* **Nell.** *door* L. 2 E.]

Col. Trust a girl for making an opportunity to spoon. Well, I'll smoke a cigar just to give them a chance. [*Lights cigar and sits L. on sofa.*]

[*Enter* **Baby** *and* **Fran.** *carrying potted flowers door* L. 1 E. **Baby** *is veiled.*]

Baby. Now, then, stupid—do you want to smash the pots? What makes you so awkward?

Fran. If you nag at me much more, I *will* smash them. You've kept it up ever since we left the florist's! This isn't my job, anyway.

Baby. Hold your tongue." [*Sniffs, smelling smoke.*] Oh there's a strange man. [*Bows.*]

Col. Dr. Lyon will be here in a moment, madam. Won't you excuse my cigar and sit down? [*Points to chair* R. *of table.*]

Baby. To whom have I the honor———?

Col. I am Dr. Lyon's uncle—Richard Lyon.

Baby. Oh!

Col. Allow me to offer you a chair. [*Places the chair.*] I'll call my nephew. [*Calls.*] Lysander—Sandy—a lady to see you. [*Sits on sofa.*]

Baby. [*Aside.*] That's pretty cool, too. [*Aloud. Taking off hat and veil.*] Francisco, carry those flowers to my room.

Fran. [*Down* L. *near door.*] Yes, ma'am. [*Aside.*] The old man doesn't know me in this rig. [*Ex. door* L. 2 E.]

Col. [*Aside.*] Francisco! Her room—the devil! It's his mother! [*Puts on glasses.*] By the living jingo! She's not at all a bad looking woman. Remarkably well preserved.

Enter **Lys.** *door* L. 2 E.]

Lys. [*Crossing down* R.] Did you call me, uncle? [*Aside*] Baby! I must get him out of the way or the jig is up! [*Aloud.*] Won't you go and wash your hands, sir?

Col. Yes—in a minute—you don't object to smoke, I hope, madam?

Baby. Not at all, sir. [*To* Lys.] See—I've got my dahlias and a couple of pots of—

Lys. [R. C.] That's right—there's nothing I'm so fond of as buttercups and daisies. [*Aside.*] Why won't she go away?

Baby. Daisies? I said dahlias. [*Arranging flowers.*]

Lys. So did I. Daisies—what an absurdity! I said gutter-pups and dahlias. [*Aside.*] I'm so rattled I don't know what I am saying. [R.]

Col. [*Aside.*] What a nice looking woman your mother is in spite of all she has gone through. So well preserved.

Lys. [*Aside.*] Yes—in alcohol— I mean in oil—no, no—I mean she is, yes.

Col. She looks remarkably fresh.

Lys. And she's fresher than she looks, a darn sight.

Col. [*Rising, confidentially.*] She hasn't forgiven me yet. She was as stiff as a poker the minute she recognized me.

Lys. You can hardly wonder at that.

Col. How very like her you are. You've got her nose and mouth, yes and her eyes.

Lys. [*Aside.*] I wish I had her neck. I'd break it.

Col. And you have her expression.

Lys. [*Aside.*] I wonder if there is any Paris green in the house?

Col. But really, it seems almost impossible that you should be her son.

Lys. I find it hard to believe it myself. [*Crosses* L. *Aside to* **Baby.**] Go to your room!

Baby. [*Aside.*] I shan't. Introduce me to your uncle over again.

Lys. What for?

Baby. Because yesterday in your excitement you said "mother" instead of "daughter."

Lys. I explained that fully when I saw him later last night.

Baby. [*Rises.*] Introduce me properly or I'll make a scene, contract or no contract.

Lys. [R. C. *Aside.*] There's a deadly glitter in her eye. She means it. [*Aloud.*] This is my Uncle Richard, you know, dear. He has been very kind to me and I want you both to forget the past and be good friends for my sake. [*Aside.*] Now go to your room. [*Hands* **Col.** *from* R. *to* L. *and pushes* **Baby** *towards door* L. 2 E., *but she passes behind him* R.]

Col. Delighted, I'm sure, madam, to——[*Not finding her* L. *crosses behind* **Lys.** R., *who passes* **Baby** L. *in front of him.*]

Baby. [L. C. *Aside to* **Lys.**] Madam! He *still* takes me for your mother.

Lys. [C. *Aside.*] Remember our contract. Not a hint of who you are.

Col. [R. C.] I've brought some playthings for little Tootsy-wootsey.

Baby. Playthings for little Tootsywootsey!

Lys. Yes, dear—Tootsywootsey. It's a Californian expression of Spanish origin. [*Aside.*] Go to your room!

Col. Brothers-in-law and sisters-in-law, the world over, have the privilege of shaking hands, and——[*Offers hand to* **Baby.** **Lys.** *takes it.*]

Baby. What does he mean?

Lys. That's an old Spanish proverb common in California. In Spain brothers-in-law and sisters-in-law *have* that privilege. [*Aside.*] Go to your *room* or you don't get that *husband.*]

Baby. You brute! [*Bows stiffly to Col. and ex. door* l. 2 e.]

Col. [r.] A fine woman, though a little eccentric. Does she like cribbage?

Lys. Like it? It's almost a vice with her. I've even heard her murmur "two for his nobs" in her sleep. [*Aside.*] She was alluding to me! [*Drops into chair* r. *of table.*]

Col. By the living jingo! If she were not my brother's widow—

Lys. Take her to the Sandwich Islands—it doesn't matter there.

Col. And to think I've hated her for thirty years! Well, I'd better get brushed up for lunch and then be off to see Dr. Soakem about my case. Just think, my boy—whenever I eat—

Lys. Exactly. Oh, it's very serious.

Col. Isn't it? I'm getting quite uneasy about it. [*Goes to* r. *door.*] Shall I wash in here?

Lys. Yes, that's the door.

Col. Tell your mother that I'll tell her all about my case over a game of cribbage.

Lys. Yes do—tell her all your symptoms. She'll be delighted and tell you all *her's.*

Col. I will. [*Ex.* r. *door.*]

Lys. How is this to end? Nellie will insist on seeing the baby, and when I pop into her arms that tender little suckling in its forty-seventh year—bang! Away she goes! [*Cigar stump thrown on balcony.*] Cuss that fellow! [*Rushes out and looks up.*] You keep out of sight, you're wise! See here, you sir, how many more snipes are you going to throw on my balcony?

Derb. I'm no prophet, don't you know.

Lys. What business have you to throw your refuse down here?

Derb. What business has your balcony under my window?

Lys. I'd like to get you stuffed and put in a glass case as the champion American hog. You're next door to a fool. [*Reentering.*]

Derb. I tumbled to that fact the very day you moved in, don't you know.

Lys. I'd like to soak you once—just *once!* [*Coming down.*] Oh for a lingering and terrible revenge—an inspiration. I've got him! Within six days I've got to find a nice, meek little husband for Baby. He shall be the victim! [*Goes up. Calls.*] Oh, captain—major judge doctor —whatever your title is.

Derb. What's the trouble, have you got another worm?

Lys. No, no!—it's all right now. Just step down stairs for five minutes to see me.

Derb. See you? I don't mind calling from here, don't you know. What have you got? Stuffed club flush, a pair of dogs, or four of a kind in bullets?

Lys. Neither. But I have a business proposition with lots of money in it for you.

Derb. Wait a minute till I get my revolver.

Lys. Oh, you won't need a gun. I'm peaceable. [*Comes down.*] That was a stroke of genius. If the fellow happens to be poor he'll be glad to get $250,000, no matter what sort of a dose he may have to take on the side. My happiness would be complete if he would take her for a wedding tour around the world in eighty years. [*Down c.*]

[**Derb.** *enters door* L. 1 E.]

Derb. [*At door, pointing revolver.*] Throw up your hands.

Lys. [*Holding up hands.*] Dashwood! The dickens! Lower that gun.

Derb. Oh no, dear boy! I've called and insist upon seeing what you've got. [*Feels* Lys. *for weapons.*] It's all right now. Drop your hands. [*Puts gun in pocket.*] Now what's your scheme? No fiction, mind.

Lys. I understand that you've been let out at Washington.

Derb. Yes—I'm a republican and had to walk the plank, don't you know.

Lys. How are you fixed?

Derb. About $10,000 in debt, dear boy.

Lys. Good!

Derb. Yes, deuced good!

Lys. Any prospects?

Derb. I had until you turned up. Nellie Goldengate.

Lys. Oh—so she was N. G. Ha, ha, ha! Then that accounts for the snipes! In your despair you are trying to suicide by smoking yourself to death.

Derb. Oh no, by Jove. You annoyed me by blighting my prospects and I was trying to play even. I did think of switching to the chewing gum girl but I can't get up the nerve.

Lys. She's chilly, anyway. Sit down. [**Derb.** *sits* R. *and* Lys. L. *of table.*]

Derb. Yes, awfully. Meantime I just sit in my window and watch for Mamey.

Lys. Mamey?

Derb. The statuesque blonde in the cafe, don't you know. On the dead quiet, old man, she's my ideal.

Lys. Hush—as the father of a family I can't listen to any such confidences.

Derb. I say, old chappie, fiction, you know! You're beginning it again. Father of a family, don't you know!

Lys. That's fact, not fiction. I wish it was. Now, would $250,000 be any object to you?

Derb. Don't talk stuff.

Lys. But I am talking stuff—two hundred and fifty thousand of long green stuff. Now, as you happen to be an old friend of mine I'll put you in the way of getting it—by the way, [*Rising.*] I have some ten-year old hand-made sour mash, as mild as milk, and as strong as mustard. [*Gets decanter, etc.*]

Derb. That's my poison—I'm desperate. [Lys. *brings down liquor on tray.*]

Lys. [*Pouring liquor.*] Try a nip.

Derb. Nip? Give me a whole pony. I feel real devilish.

Lys. Try that. Here's looking at you. [*Drinks.*]

Derb. [*Gulps liquor. It burns him.*] Oh, I say—my throat, oh, by Jove!

Lys. Good, isn't it? [*Sits.*]

Derb. Yes—awfully. [*Choking.*]

Lys. Have another. [*Pours.*]

Derb. Not on your life, dear boy. Now about this $250,000. [*Lights cigar.*]

Lys. I have a wife for you.

Derb. The deuce you have!

Lys. Charming woman—refined, accomplished, draws, sings, plays——

Derb. Excuse me, old man. [*Rising.*] I must be going, really——

Lys. She has $250,000 of her own——

Derb. Fairy tales—I know you too well, dear boy.

Lys. I'll give you proof positive in a minute. Here, have another nip, it'll do you good. [*Pours liquor.*]

Derb. Here's a go at the $250,000 girl. [*Drinks.*]

Lys. You can marry her in three days without any trouble.

Derb. That settles Mamey—her eye is out and—[*Sits down.*]

Lys. Hush—as the father of a family, you know—

Derb. That's twice you've sprung that. Explain—what father? Whose family?

Lys. You'll know in a minute. Of course with $250,000 you don't expect a Lillian Russell.

Derb. Well, of course—I don't you know—

Lys. Of course not. You're a sensible man. [*Aside.*] Brainless ninkumpoop! [*Aloud.*] And you wouldn't look for sweet sixteen—this girl is of age and can do what she likes with her money.

Derb. Oh, I say—you want to steer me up against some infernal old hen.

Lys. Not at all.

Derb. Describe her, dear boy.

Lys. A Greek profile—all intellect—and an expression worth $250,000.

Derb. Expression is everything, after all, dear boy. Who is the lady? [*Helps himself to liquor ad. lib.*]

Lys. My daughter.

Derb. [*Almost dropping decanter.*] What? I thought you'd given up lying!

Lys. I have. To be strictly accurate I should have said my step-daughter. I'm a widower.

Derb. She must be awfully young to marry, don't you know.

Lys. Oh no she isn't—not very *much* too young.

Derb. I'd like to see the little thing.

Lys. Well, she isn't exactly little, either.

Derb. Good—here's to her. I admire big women. [*Drinks.*] Why, Mamey is five feet eleven without her—

Lys. Hush! As the father of a family—

Derb. Eh? Oh! Exactly! Well, you offer me $250,000 and a young girl.

Lys. I didn't say a *young girl*—I said my step-daughter. Let us be accurate, for I am very tender of my reputation as a truthful man.

Derb. I say, old chappie, you have reformed, haven't you? Anyway, if she's your step-daughter she can't be very old.

Lys. [*Going up. Putting away decanter, etc. Aside.*] Oh, can't she!

Derb. Trot her out and let's look at her. [*Rising and going up.*]

Lys. Sure thing—only throw away that cigar, won't you?

Derb. What for?

Lys. Oh, a first interview, you know—it would hardly do.

Derb. Then there it goes. [*Throws cigar.*]

Lys. That's right—keep it up. My balcony's used to it. [*Drawing him down stage.*]

Derb. Mamey doesn't mind a little smoke.

Lys. Hush—as the father of a family—

Derb. That's all right, old man, but Mamey's a mighty fine girl and I'm stuck on her. [*Ex.* **Lys.** *door* L. 2 E.] You never saw such hair, such eyes, such a form—Mamey's all right. [*Looks around. Intoxicated.*] Why, he's gone—good stuff, that sour mash I'll hit it again. [*Begins to wabble up stage as* Lys. *reenters with* **Baby.**] I guess I won't—I've had enough. [*Wheels around and comes down* R.]

Lys. [*Aside to* **Baby.**] Now cast down your eyes and keep your profile turned to him. You gain fifty per cent. by being seen in profile. He'll only see half of her. [*Crossing with her down* C.]

Derb. [*Very whobbly.*] Derby, old chappie, brace up. [*With back to* **Lys.**]

Lys. [*Places her* C. *and goes* R. C. *Aside.*] He'll pull that gun on me when he sees her.

Derb [*Aside.*] I'm almost too full to face the poor innocent young thing. [*Sees her and staggers back.*] Am I only full or have I got the jim jams?

Lys. Allow me to introduce you to my daughter—Miss Baby. Mr. Dashwood, my dear. [*No matter where* **Derb.** *goes* **Baby** *always remains* C. *and keeps her side view turned to him.*]

Derb. [*Aside.*] You must have been married at two years old.

Lys. I *was* quite young.

Derb. But—but she's older than you are.

Lys. Never mind her age. She has $250,000 and if you want to help her spend it, wire in.

Derb. I will—but I wish I'd got that other drink. [*Crosses* C. *to* **Baby.**] Allow me to express and—believe me sincere in saying, don't you know, it is impossible— [*Aside.*] Oh, it *is* impossible. [*Crosses* R. *to* **Lys.**] I can't do it. She's too much for me.

Baby. [*Aside.*] Sweet little man—how agitated he seems.

Lys. [*Goes to her* C.] Baby, the solemn moment has at length arrived when I must prepare myself to part with you and assist in establishing you in life. [*Aside.*] Turn your profile.

Derb. [R.] That moment is forty years late, by Jove!

Lys. Mr. Derby Dashwood, ninth assistant something or other at Washington, can no longer conceal the love which you have inspired.

Derb. [*Crosses to him and pulls him* R.] Hold on—hold on I say——I——[*Aside with* **Lys.**]

Baby. [C. *aside.*] Ninth assistant something or other at Washington—how sweet.

Derb. Upon my soul, old chappie—I *am* dead broke but I wouldn't marry her for a million.

Baby. [*Aside to* **Lys.**] What was that he said, papa?

Lys. [*Crossing back to her.*] He was regretting his poverty and wishing for your sake that he was worth a million.

Baby. How sweet to be loved for one's self alone. Oh, Mr. Dashwood, papa's wishes are my law. I accept.

Lys. Lucky fellow! She accepts! [*Dragging him to her.*]

Derb. [R.] Hold on—hold on—I say you must allow me, really—

Lys. Oh, of course. Now's your time—tackle her boldly. [*Aside.*] Oh, if I could only get another drink into him! [*Aloud.*] Remember, $250,000.

Derb. That's all right, but candidly, don't you know—how old is she?

Lys. Two hundred and fifty thousand.

Derb. She looks her age. No matter—I'll tackle her boldly. [*Crosses to Baby.*] Allow me to express and believe me sincere in saying—aw—aw— don't you know—my two hundred and fifty thousand—I never—excuse me—you have made a complete sour mash—aw—pardon me—[*Crosses L.*] I'm rattled—I can't do it—I must go and think it over. [*Goes up.*]

Lys. [*To Baby.*] He's agitated, he doesn't know what he's saying. [*Aside.*] He's drunk as a fly. [*Goes up to Derb.*] What are you going to do?

Derb. I'll—I'll play you a game of billiards—come on. [*Pulling him C.*]

Lys. [*Aside.*] If I leave him he's lost. [*Aloud.*] Of course I will—but you haven't said good bye to your intended.

Derb. Oh, haven't I? That's a fact. [*Comes down a little to Baby.*] My intended two hundred and—I mean, I've a good mind to—a—and yet I—adieu. [*Kisses hand to her. Aside.*] It's no use—I can't do it, I really can't—come along. [*Takes Lys. arm.*]

Lys. We'll be back directly, dear. [Baby *follows kissing her hand to* Derb.] Go to your room and stay there or you'll lose him. [*Ex. with Derb. C.*]

Baby. [*Sits R. of table.*] What a charming little man—and how he worships me! He became quite incoherent, but I understood him. Oh, I'm just madly in love—our meeting was so romantic.

[*Enter* Col. *door R. crosses to door* L. 2 E. *and knocks.*]

Col. Come along, Nellie—the little dear must be awake by this time. We'll show her the pretty things we've brought her.

Nell. [*Entering door* L. 2 E.] I've got my little hood. [*They cross down R.*]

Baby. [*Aside.*] Papa's uncle. I thought he'd gone. But who is *she.*

Col. [R. C. *to* Nell.] Lysander's mother. She's a famous cribbage player. I'll introduce you. [*Bows.*] Madam, allow me to present Miss Nellie Goldengate of California—his intended wife. [*Nell is* R.]

Baby. [*Rises and bows stiffly.*] Indeed, sir; whose intended wife?

Col. Why, your son's, of course.

Baby. My son's! [*Horrified and indignant.*] I have *no* son.

Col. and Nell. No son!

Baby. I'm an unmarried woman.

Col. Unmarried! Another of his lies. Accept my sincere apologies. I am really mortified at my blunder. We thought you were the grandma.

Baby. Grandma! Whose grandma!

Col. Why, little Tootsywootsey's to be sure. Is she awake yet?

Baby. Tootsywootsey?

Col. Yes—the little girl—my nephew's child.

Baby. Sir, *I* am your nephew's child.

Nell. Good gracious!

Col. What! You little Tootsywootsey? Oh by Jove, by Jupiter, by jingo, by the *living* jingo! [*Stamping with rage.*]

Nell. This simply out-herods Herod! I'll never forgive him—never, never! [*Sinks into chair.*]

Col. [*Suddenly changing.*] And I was going to give you this for a husband! [*Jumping the toy, which he takes from pocket. Crosses* L.]

Nell. And I brought you this cute little—[*Dangles hood.*]

Baby. Cute little what? Let's see it.

Nell. Oh, it's nothing. [*Puts it hastily in her pocket. Sits on sofa.*]

Col. Didn't he introduce you to me yesterday as his mother?

Baby. Didn't he explain his slip of the tongue when he saw you later in the evening?

Col. He did not.

Baby. Cruel, cruel papa to treat me so!

Col. [L.] Inveterate, chronic liar to treat us all so!

Nell. Don't be *too* severe on the poor fellow.

Col. Oho! So you are going to forgive him!

Nell. Never!

Col. Neither will I.

Nell. But it's your duty to forgive seventy times seven.

Col. Not him—he's my nephew—not my brother.

Baby. [*Aside.*] Heavens! I've broken my contract with

papa! Oh my husband, my husband that was to be!

Col. Well, I'll forgive him if you will. [*Sits L. of table. To Baby.*] Let me see—what is our present relationship? You are my grand-niece by marriage and will soon be Nellie's daughter.

Nell. [*Rising excitedly.*] Not if Nellie knows herself! [*Crosses to C.*]

Col. Nonsense, my dear! You are going to marry her papa so I don't see how you can avoid becoming her mama.

Nell. [C.] I her mama? Not in a thousand years!

Baby. [*Aside.*] And this is all on my account! Boo hoo boo hoo I've lost a husband and it's all my own fault. Boohoo, boohoo! [*Ex. R. 2 E.*]

Col. She's crying. Poor girl.

Nell. Girl? How soon do you expect her to bud into womanhood?

Col. Oh, she's not so old—rather advanced to be one's grandniece, perhaps, but for all that a very charming woman. [*Looks at watch.*] But dear me, how late it's getting! There doesn't seem to be any immediate prospect of lunch so I'll be off to see my specialist. [*Rises.*]

Nell. I'll go with you.

Col. No dear—you can't be present at my consultation, and it's only in the next block, anyway. You stop here and chat with your new daughter.

Nell. New daughter! I tell you I'll never, never—

Col. Don't be rash! You'll forgive him and she'll be your daughter sooner or later, so the sooner you make her acquaintance the better.

Nell. Never! The idea of a daughter old enough to be my grandmother! [*Sinks into chair R. of table.*]

Col. Tut, tut, tut—just think over it. I'll be back soon. [*Ex. door L. 1 E.*]

[*Enter Lys. C.*]

Lys. I can't bring that confounded idiot to the point. He's gone to get another drink and take ten minutes more to make up his mind.

Nell. [*Seeing him, rises.*] Oh, so you have returned.

Lys. [*Coming down.*] Yes, dear, here I am at last. I hope my absence hasn't annoyed you?

Nell. Oh no! I've had a real nice time!

Lys. I'm glad of that. Don't you think I'm comfortably settled?

Nell. You *are* settled—finally.

Lys. Why, Nell—what's gone wrong? [*Tries to put arm around her.*]

Nell. [c.] Don't touch me, sir! I have just seen little Tootsy-wootsey.

Lys. [R. C.] I *am* settled. [*Aloud.*] Little Tootsywootsey —ha, ha, ha!

Nell. You may think little Tootsywootsey is funny, sir. I *don't.* and if you imagine that I will submit to be called "mama" by an elderly lady like that you are greatly mistaken.

Lys. I don't blame you—of course not. But it's all right—only wait a bit. I'll get rid of her.

Nell. Get rid of her?

Lys. Yes, yes—it's all right. I tell you. I'm going to marry her off.

Nell. So that her children may call me grandma! Never! [*Goes up c.*]

Lys. Worse and worse and more of it!

Nell. Dr. Lyon, I am very sorry, but under existing circumstances our marriage is impossible. [*Going L.*]

Lys. [*Down R. C. Despairingly.*] But what can I do?

Nell. *I* don't know. But I *do* know that no power on earth can induce me to marry you so long as that full sized freak of nature is galloping loose around the world.

Lys. But I can't get her called in by act of congress.

Nell. That is *your* business. *Mine* is to seek a change of scene and try to forget the events of the past two days.

Lys. [*Going up to her.*] But Nellie, dear Nellie—you admit that it isn't my fault.

Nell. No. It is our mutual misfortune.

Lys. Then let us share it.

Nell. Share *her?* Thank you. I know when I have enough! [*Ex. door L. 2 E.*]

[*Col. enters door L. 1 E.*]

Col. Well, sir, what have you got to say for yourself? [*Crosses R.*]

Lys. [*Comes down c.*] I'm all broken up. Nellie has thrown me down. [*Sits R. of table.*]

Col. Serves you right. I thought you made a full confession last night and swore off lying. [*Sits on sofa.*]

Lys. So I did. But I knew that if Nellie ever saw that frost bitten cyclone before our wedding it was all up between us. You seemed so anxious for our marriage and I was so eager to obey your wishes that I determined to keep her suppressed if I could.

Col. Your motives render your offense more tolerable, but you didn't figure close enough. You can't forsee such accidents.

Lys. Your visit *was* an accident of course. It wasn't poor

Baby's fault. She has her good points.

Col. I should say so! She's a very superior woman and if she really had been your mother you might have been justly proud of her.

Lys. [*Aside.*] I might have been proud of her as a mother— why shouldn't I be proud of her as an aunt? There's a scheme for your life!

. **Col.** It's a lucky thing for you that I vented my rage on that scoundrelly specialist, and so hadn't steam enough left to blow you up.

Lys. What has he done?

Col. I never heard of a doctor doing such a thing before.

Lys. You don't mean to tell me he has been curing somebody?

Col. No—not that. He's gone and where do you think?

Lys. To Dwight?

Col. No sir! To Chicago to be treated by a specialist. A specialist sick himself! Did you ever hear of anything so utterly idiotic? Here have I come all the way from Frisco to look after him and he's gone all the way to Chicago to look after himself.

Lys. Shameful selfishness! But it gives me a chance to renew the offer of my services.

Col. I'm afraid of experiments.

Lys. I'm no experimentalist when it comes to treating mental maladies and intellectual disorders.

Col. That's what mine is—an intellectual disorder. Imagine, now, whenever I eat—

Lys. Show me your pulse. [*Crosses to him.*]

Col. There it is. [*Sticks out tongue.*]

Lys. That isn't your pulse.

Col. That's the way Dr. Briggs begins.

Lys. Oh, he's an old woman. [*Feels pulse, watch in hand.*] As I expected—frequent—intermittent—inconsistent—indolent— eloquent!

Col. Don't flatter me.

Lys. How old are you?

Col. Sixty-four last birthday.

Lys. I thought so. Had the measles?

Col. Yes.

Lys. I thought so. Mumps?

Col. Never.

Lys. I thought not. Now I don't want to alarm you—can you stand a shock? [*Taking him c.*]

Col. I'm a dead man. Speak out.

Lys. Did you ever have the stethoscope applied?

Col. Never.

Lys. [c.] I thought not. Briggs always was an old woman. [*Sounds him on chest and back, ad lib.*]

Col. Well, is it dangerous?

Lys. Fatal unless promptly treated. You have a chronic complication of epidemical sensations acting through the nervous tissues, associated with the diaphanous cuticles covering the metempsychosis of your periosteum.

Col. [*Crosses L. c.*] Lord have mercy! Am I so bad as that? Which is my periosteum? Where is it situated?

Lys. Everywhere.

Col. That's it. That's where it strikes me—everywhere. Is there no remedy?

Lys. Out of nine patients, I've lost eight.

Col. I'm doomed!

Lys. On the ninth I tried a new treatment and cured him.

Col. Hope revives. What's the treatment?

Lys. You'd never submit to it.

Col. I would—I *will*. My boy, I don't want to die for your sake.

Lys. It's medicine for a horse.

Col. Drastic?

Lys. Number nine was sorry he didn't die.

Col. What did you do to him?

Lys. Like yourself, he was an old bachelor.

Col. Poor devil!

Lys. I married him.

Col. Married him!

Lys. It was his last chance. What is the cause of those sensations here and all down here? The nerves. When the nerves are out of order who can best soothe and calm them into their proper state of repose? A wife! What is the best medicine to attack them with? Cribbage!

Col. Wonderful! I'm off for Frisco to-night! [*Crosses R.*]

Lys. What for?

Col. Medicine for a horse.

Lys. Delays are dangerous.

Col. But I don't know anybody here.

Lys. You must be blind. Have you beheld unmoved the agitation of a fresh young heart palpitating within a yard of your callous bosom? A heart full of love and cribbage—I mean devotion!

Col. What! Do you mean Prudence?

Lys. [c.] Hush—brush up your hair and straighten your tie.

[*Enter* **Baby** *door* L. 2 E., *in different dress.* To **Baby**.] Come here my child. Now, cast your eyes down and turn your profile. My pet, the solemn moment has arrived when it becomes my duty to assist in establishing you in life.

Baby. [L. C.] You said that before.

Lys. It has arrived for the second time to-day. Turn your profile. This is the husband I have chosen for you. [*Stepping from between them.*] Uncle, your cure.

Baby. What!

Col. [R. C.] Eh?

Lys. Tableau!

Baby. [*Aside.*] Oh, papa, he's too old.

Lys, [*Aside.*] Come off! He's only a little over fifty and you know you are considerably over—

Baby. That'll do—I won't have him. I want my Dashwood.

Col. [*Drags* **Lys.** *aside* R.[But my boy—she's your daughter. How can I marry my grand-niece? I'd get arrested.

Lys. She's only your grand-niece by marriage—no kin to me and therefore none to you. You're *all right,* and you don't have to take her to the Sandwich Islands, either.

Col. But isn't she rather———

Lys. Not at all. Why, she isn't forty-eight yet. A trifle passe, perhaps, for a grand-niece, but positively juvenile for a wife. You're nearly sixty-five—there's no disparity--and think of the cribbage there is in store for you.

Col. But, Sandy—

Lys. Think of your periosteum.

Col. [R. C. *Aside.*] I stand between death and marriage. It's an awful predicament—the devil on one side and the deep, deep sea on the other. [*To* **Lys.**] Do you think she could love me?

Lys. She could love anything. She's dead gone on you.

Baby Stop, papa! Sir, I am much flattered by your proposal but our marriage is impossible. I am already engaged to a high government official. [*Sits* L. *of table.*]

Lys. [*To* **Col.**] Leave her to me. [*Crosses* L. *to* **Baby.**] Don't throw away your chances. Dashwood has turned you down.

Baby. I don't believe it. He loves me.

Lys. Besides, he lives in Washington and you would be separated from your doating papa. My child, my child--it would break my heart. [*Emotionally.*]

Baby. Don't break down, papa. I'll write you by every mail.

Lys. [*Aside.*] What a treat! [*Aloud.*] But I tell you he's gone.

Baby. My heart tells me he'll return.

Lys. Your heart's an old twaddle and doesn't know its business. [**Derb.** *dishevelled and unsteady is led in* C. *by* **Prud.**]

Derb. How do, Miss Gol'ngate –[hic] –ah there, colonel. [*To* **Lys.**] I've made up my mind, don't you know. *Coming down* C.]

Baby. [*Aside.*] I knew he'd come.

Derb. It's all right, I tell you. [*Drops handkerchief and attempts during the following speeches to pick it up without tipping over.*] I've made up—excuse me, my mind.

Lys. To refuse?

Derb. No—to accept. [**Lys.** *crosses* R.] Who could resist her (hic) $250,000? [*Crosses* L. *to* **Baby.**] Allow me to express and believe me sincere. [*She turns her full face to him.*] No—it's worse than I thought—I can't do it—I'll go out and get another drink. [*Staggers up* C. **Prud.** *stops him and they talk in pantomime.*]

Col. They've quarreled.

Lys. She has turned him down for you. Lucky man. Just call her Baby and she is yours. [*Crosses* L. *to* **Baby.**]

Col. What! Refused that young sprig for me? [*Goes* L. C.] Oh Baby!

Lys. [*To* **Baby.**] Now don't be a fool. It's your last chance. Call him Richard and he is yours.

Baby. Richard—there's my hand.

Col. My little Tootsywootsey! [*Conducting her* C.]

Baby. My pretty Dick! [*They embrace.*]

Lys. *Crosses behind them to* C.] Touching spectacle. [**Nell** *enters* L. 2 *door.*] Bless you my children.

Nell. Why, what's all this?

Lys. It's all settled.

Nell. [L. C.] What's all settled?

Baby. [R. C.] Everything, dear mama.

Lys. [C.] Baby, dear—you mustn't call her mama now.

Nell. I should say *not.*

Lys. Now see, dear, if you marry me you will be her niece, because she is going to marry Uncle Dick. You wouldn't have her for a daughter, but how does she strike you as an aunt?

Nell. [*To* **Col.**] Do you mean to say you are going to marry —— ?

Col. [R.] For my periosteum, dear. I've got to do it. I wish you'd forgive my scamp of a nephew and go and do likewise.

Nell. For *my* periosteum?

Prud. [*Coming down* R. *with* **Derb.** *whom she has straightened up.*] Nellie, dear, congratulate me.

Derb. Yes—it's catching, don't you know.

[*Enter* Kitty *with* **Fran.** *door* L. 2 E.]

Kitty. [*Down* L. *corner.*] We've come to give notice, sir. Francisco's going to open a saloon.

Nell. [C. *with* **Lys.**.] Well, I suppose the only thing left for me as a dutiful girl is to obey the commands of my guardian.

Col. Until you get a husband to order you about.

Lys. And she's got one under contract to be delivered f. o. b. this day week.

Lysander.   Nellie.

Derby.   Prudence.

Col. Lyon.   Baby.   **Francisco.   Kitty.**

Curtain.

A MODERN ANANIAS,

Comedy in Three Acts

BY

JOHN A. FRASER, Jr.

Four male, four female characters. Two interior, one exterior scenes. Modern society cotumes. Plays two and one half hours. This is a screaming farcial comedy, which depends upon the wit and humor of its lines no less than upon the drollery and absurdity of its situations for the shrieks of laughter it invariably provokes. Unlike most farcical comedies, "A Modern Ananias" has an ingeniously complicated plot, which maintains a keen dramatic interest untill the fall of the last curtain. The scenery, if necessary, may be reduced to a garden scene and an interior. Every character in the piece is full of comedy of the most humorous description, and one of them, a fat old maid, may be performed by a male somewhat after the fashion of "Charley's Aunt." The climaxes are hilariously funny, and each of the three acts is punctuated with laughs from beginning to end. Amateurs will find nothing more satisfactory in the whole range of the comic drama than this up-to-date comedy-farce by J. A. Fraser, Jr. The fullest stage directions accompany the book, including all the "crosses" and positions, pictures, etc. Price, 25 cents.

'TWIXT LOVE AND MONEY,

Comedy Drama in Four Acts

BY

JOHN A. FRASER, Jr.

Eight male, three female characters. Plays two and one-half hours. Three interior scenes. Costumes of the day. This charming domestic comedy drama of the present day bids fair to rival, both with professionals and amateurs, the success of "Hazel Kirke." The scene is laid in a little village on the coast of Maine, and the action is replete with dramatic situations which "play themselves." The story is intensely interesting and, in these days of Frenchy adaptations and "problem" plays, delightfully pure; while the moral that love brings more happiness than does money—is plainly pointed without a single line of preaching. No such romatic interest has been built up around a simple country heroines since the production of "Hazel Kirke" and "May Blossom" years ago. The play is in four acts, and as the scenery is easy to manage it is particularly well adapted for the use of amateurs. There are three female parts, two of them comic characters, and eight males, two of whom supply the comedy. The dressing is all modern and the piece forms a full evening's entertainment. The author, J. A. Fraser, Jr., has been highly successful as a dramatist for the professional stage, having written. "The Noble Outcast" "Edelweiss." "The Merry Cobbler." The Train Wreckers," "A Delicate Question." "A Modern Ananias." "Becky Bliss, the Circus Girl," and many other well-known and successful plays. "Twixt Love and Money" has been carefully revised by the author for the amateur stage. Price 25 cents.

The Dramatic Publishing Company, Chicago.

THE MERRY COBBLER.
Comedy Drama in Four Acts
BY
JOHN A. FRASER, Jr.

Six male, five female characters. Two interior, two exterior scenes. Modern costumes. Time of play, one hour and forty-five minutes. This refined, yet laughter-making comedy, in which John R. Cumpson starred successfully for several seasons, has been carefully revised by the author for the amateur stage. This romantic story of a German imigrant boy in New Orleans, who falls in love with, and finally marries, a dashing Southern belle, is one of the cleanest and daintiest in the whole repertoire of the minor stage. In addition to the Merry Cobbler himself, who is one of the type the late J. K. Emmet so loved to portray, there are five other male characters, five female parts and very short parts for two little girls. Had the piece been originally written for the use of amateurs, it could not have been happier in its results, its natural and mirth-provoking comedy combined with a strong undercurrent of heart-interest, rendering it a vehicle with which even inexperienced actors are sure to be seen at their best. The scenic effects are of the simplest description and the climaxes, while possessing the requisite amount of "thrill" are very easy to handle. This piece has been seen in all the larger cities of the Union during the past four seasons, and is now placed within the reach of amateurs for the first time. J. A. Fraser, Jr., author of "The Merry Cobbler," and a score of other successful plays, has prepared elaborate instructions for its production by amateur players. Price, 25 cents.

A DELICATE QUESTION,
Comedy Drama in Four Acts
BY
JOHN A. FRASER, Jr.

Nine male, three female characters. One exterior, two interior scenes. Modern costumes. Plays two hours. If a play presenting an accurate picture of life in the rural districts is required, in which every character has been faithfully studied from life, nothing better for the use of amateurs than "A Delicate Question" can be recommended. The story is utterly unlike that of any other play and deals with the saloon, which it handles without gloves and at the same time without a single line of sermonizing. What "Ten Nights in a Barroom" was to the public of a past generation, "A Delicate Question" is destined to be to the present, although it is far from being exactly what is known as a "temperance play." The plot is intensely interesting, the pathetic scenes full of beauty, because they are mental photographs from nature, and the comedy is simply uproariously funny. The parts, very equally balanced. The scenic effects are quite simple, and by a little ingenuity the entire piece may be played in a kitchen scene. The climaxes are all as novel as they are effective and the dialogue is as natural as if the characters were all real people. The author, J. A. Fraser, Jr., considers this one of his greatest successes. Price, 25 cents.

The Dramatic Publishing Company, Chicago.

Aroused at Last.

COMEDY IN ONE ACT. BY

MARY KYLE DALLAS.

Characters, four male and four female, to say nothing of the dog. Time of representation about forty minutes. One interior scene, extremely æsthetic style.

Price, -   -   -   -   15 cents.

SYNOPSIS OF INCIDENTS:

Mr. Pondicherry presents his wife with a diamond ring, engraved with the words, "Never Once," which he explains to mean, that he has never had occasion to be jealous of her. Demonstrates what he would do if he were aroused. Timely entrance of Celeste. Arrival of Cousin Hetabel Wiggins and her brother Jackson from Toadfish Point. "Meestaire and Messes Vandernoodle ask if you are home." "I'll stand, thanks. It winkles one's knees less." Jackson rescues his porkmantle. "I've got most of grandpa's things; these pants was his'n." "Bow-wow was lost for hours, and I was utterly prostrated. His mamma would like to let him bite the nasty elevator boy, zere little angel." Catastrophe of the lunch things. "I'm prohibition when I'm to hum, but this is bully cider—champagne you call it." "Here's to us and our folks." Hetabel on a tour of investigation through Mrs. P.'s secretary. "Aha! now I can show Packingham Pondicherry what a mistake he made when he choose Pamela Kidd instead of me." "What! a sea serpent in my bosom!" "Speak, woman, speak." "Avaunt." "I hold the proof of your duplicity in my hands." P. aroused at last. Vandernoodle's awful peril. Timely interference of Celeste. "Written by a driveling idiot." "Of all brazen critters." "Bring me my Bow-wow, he's all I have to love me now." "Mr. Pondicherry, have you lost all memory of your own love-letters?" "Good Heavens! What an idiot I have made of myself." "Open another bottle of cider." Miss Hetabal and her brother shown the door. Happy reconciliation all around.

A Pair of Artists.

AN ORIGINAL COMEDY IN THREE ACTS, BY

EFFIE W. MERRIMAN.

Characters, four male, three female. Time, one hour and three-fourths.

Price, - - - - 15 cents.

SYNOPSIS OF INCIDENTS.

ACT I. SCENE I. Irving Richmond's apartments. Irving confesses to his old college chum that he is in love. Charles very much against marriage sympathizes deeply in his affliction. The poor artist's scheme.

SCENE II. Scott farmhouse. Uncle Tom and Gertie teaching each other to waltz. Aunt Kate mends chair, meanwhile delivering lecture on "Woman Suffrage." Lillian's letter to Irving intercepted by Aunt Kate and sent to Papa. Irving upon the scene in guise of farm-hand. Caught love-making by Willie.

ACT II. SCENE, sitting-room Scott farmhouse. A summer boarder (Charlie); also a poor artist. Charlie shells peas. Gertie's suspicions that Charlie is Irving. Charlie led lively dance by Gertie. Gertie's portrait painted by Charlie a sad failure. Examination of Willie's mental condition unsatisfactory. Johnny-jump-up determines to become a pansy. Gertie's revenge on Charlie. Charlie argues with Aunt Kate and gets himself into trouble. Willie's astounding revelation at the supper table. Confusion!

ACT III. SCENE, same as for ACT II. Charlie as a moral teacher to the young not a success. Another discovery by Willie. Aunt Kate writes to Papa. Charlie and Willie take a trip to the city. Elopement of Lillian and Irving. Uncle Tom tells Gertie a story. "I ain't crying, Uncle Tom,—I-I peeled onions for dinner yesterday—Oh! I wish I could die." Charlie back disguised as Lillian's papa. Gertie's involuntary confession. Uncle Tom discovers that Charlie is the son of an old friend. Charlie's opinions regarding marriage greatly changed. Mr. S. takes a new stand. "It means, madam, that hereafter I am master in my own house." Willie and Irving and Lillian back again. Everybody happy.

CHILDREN'S PLAYS

The object of publishing these little plays is to provide a series that require one scene only in each piece and which will occupy about 15 to 25 minutes in performance. They can all be thoroughly recommended as the simplest plays for children ever published. PRICE, 15 cents each.

The Fairy Blossom. 3 males, 3 females. Scene, a King's Chamber. The Fairy Blossom belonging to the queen has been stolen and the king vows he will severely punish the thief. Carlo is accused, but his betrothed wife Lena will not allow him to be sacrificed, as she plucked the flower to comfort her sick sister. The king, who had complained about having nothing to do, then learns that his alms have not been properly distributed among the poor in a proper manner and resolves to look after them himself.

A Home Fairy. 2 males, 2 females. Scene, a Parlor. Bertie Egerton and his wife are very poor and cannot get work. Their little daughter Lily is desirous of doing something to help them. The proprietor of a theatre, Cecil Vane, arrives and offers to make Lily a fairy in the pantomime, to fill the place of one who is ill. Lily's mother happens to be Vane's long lost daughter and they are happily re-united

A King in Disguise. 5 males, 1 female. Scene, a Cottage Room. This is the story of King Alfred and the cakes, his sojourn at the neat-herd's cottage, where news is brought to him of the overthrow of the Danes.

The Lady Cecil. 1 male, 4 females. Scene, a Room. A nurse brings her own child up as the Lady Cecil, the real Lady Cecil being lost when an infant. They have a handmaid, Clare, to whom the nurse is cruel, but she is beloved by Cecil. A fairy appears and pronounces Clare to be the child that was lost. Lord Hilary has courted Lady Cecil, but vows the change will not make any difference in his affections.

The Little Folks' Work. 2 males, 3 females. Scene, a Kitchen. Three little children resolve to help their father and mother in household duties; they make terrible mistakes, but their parents are satisfied with their goodwill and loving help.

The Magician and the Ring. 3 males, 2 females. Scene, a Room The Lady Trevor has lost a valuable ring. She seeks the aid of a magician to find it. He discovers that the servants have taken it and he is enabled to restore it.

A Midsummer Frolic. 2 males, 2 females. Scene, a Wood. Percy believes in fairies. His companions play a trick upon him, dressing up and making him think he is on enchanted ground.

Prince or Peasant. 2 males, 2 females. Scene, a Road. Prince Claud has been betrothed in infancy to Princess Brenda, but the Prince, tired of Court ceremonies, disguises as a peasant in order to seek someone of sterling worth in humble life. The Princess does the same, they meet and exchange rings and afterward in their Court attire they recognize in each other the peasant they have already encountered and fallen in love with.

Princess Marguerite's Choice. 5 males, 3 females. Scene, a Room. The Princess Marguerite is visited by various knights to solicit her hand in marriage. They offer her wealth, power and valor, but her choice rests upon Sir Innocent, who can offer her nothing but a spotless name and a loving heart.

Snowwhite. 4 males 2 females. Scene, a Room. The queen is jealous of Snowwhite's beauty and instructs a servant to take her into a wood and slay her. The servant pretends this has been done and Snowwhite falls into the hands of the dwarfs. The queen's magic glass telling her that Snowwhite still lives, she dresses in disguise, and twice attempts to poison her step-daughter. Her plans are frustrated, she repents and Snowwhite is united to Prince Florimel.

The Sleepers Awakened. 3 males, 3 females. Scene, a Room. Abou Hassan, the Sultan's favorite, and his wife, Nouzhatoul, are hard up. In order to obtain money he tells the Sultan that his wife is dead, while Nouzhatoul tells Zobeide, the Sultan's wife, that her husband is dead. The Sultan and his wife quarrel as to which is deceased and come to find out, whereupon Abou and Nouzhatoul both pretend to be lifeless. The Sultan offering a thousand gold pieces to know which died first, Abou jumps up and claims that he did. The Sultan is so pleased with their joke that he forgives them.

The Three Fairy Gifts. 2 males, 6 females. Scene, a Wood. A fairy queen grants a gift to the three maidens, Cynthia, Violet and Vera. The first chooses wealth, the second beauty, while Vera desires the power to make others happy. Cynthia and Violet are led into trouble by their gifts and beseech the fairy to take them away, but Vera is the means of teaching them how they should profit by their good fortune.

The Two Sisters. A bright little children's play in one act for 4 female characters.

THE DEESTRICK SKULE

--OF--

FIFTY YEARS AGO

"The Deestrick Skule" has been given in scores of towns, and everywhere with success. The manual gives full instructions for getting up the "Deestrick Skule." It contains the questions and answers for the various classes, hints on costume, several "Compositions and "pieces" for the latter part of the entertainment, a parting poetical "Tribe-ute," from the "Maw" of two pairs of twins, and the speech of the "Head Committee Man."

"One of the best entertainments of the kind it has been my pleasure to attend—FLORENCE LEE in *Good Housekeeping*.

Sent postpaid on receipt of price, 50 cents.

SOCIALS.

BY EFFIE W. MERRIMAN.

"With a view to providing societies or clubs devices both for entertainment and for making money for worthy objects, Effie W. Merriman, a well known writer of children's books, has completed a collection of schemes for socials, which meet a long felt want. A church needs furnishing, a poor family needs assistance, a new organ is wanted, a school library is to be started, a hospital calls for assistance and the question arises what can be got up that will be new and entertaining. To reply to this the suggestions in this book are made. Many of them possess novel features and while simple would be apt to provide plenty of amusement as well as money.—*Hartford Post*.

"This little book supplies a long felt want on the part of societies, clubs, benevolent associations and other organizations for novelties and entertainments.

"More than a score of amusing socials and other entertainments are described in such plain and concise terms that no one of average ability could be other than successsful in their management."—*Chicago Globe*.

Sent postpaid on receipt of price, 50 cents.

THE DRAMATIC PUBLISHING COMPANY.
CHICAGO.

PLAYS

WE keep in stock one of the largest and best assorted lines of plays to be found in the country.

We can furnish any play published. Individuals and societies interested in this class of publications should first examine our lists before ordering elsewhere.

Full descriptive catalogue, giving titles, number of characters, time required for production, etc., will be sent free on application.

THE DRAMATIC PUBLISHING COMPANY,

358 Dearborn Street,

CHICAGO.